MW01120143

We are peace
We are joy —

Barbara Aleghmush

March 31, 2009

THE
Time
HAS COME
THE BOOK *of* GRACE

BARBARA OLEYNICK

THE TIME HAS COME: THE BOOK OF GRACE, PART ONE
PUBLISHED BY SYNERGY BOOKS
2100 Kramer Lane, Suite 300
Austin, Texas 78758

For more information about our books, please write to us, call
512.478.2028, or visit our website as www.bookpros.com.

Printed and bound in Hong Kong. All rights reserved. No part of this
book may be reproduced in any form or by any electronic or mechanical
means including information storage and retrieval systems without
permission in writing from the copyright holder, except by a reviewer,
who may quote brief passages in review.

ISBN: 978-0-9755922-5-0
ISBN: 0-9755922-5-4

Copyright© 2005 by Barbara Oleynick

Publisher's Cataloging-in-Publication
(Provided by Quality Books, Inc.)

Oleynick, Barbara.
    The time has come / Barbara Oleynick.
    p. cm. — (The book of Grace)
    LCCN 2005922500
    ISBN-13: 978-0-9755922-5-0
    ISBN-10: 0-9755922-5-4

1. Orphans—Fiction. 2. God—Fiction. 3. Millennium
(Eschatology)—Fiction.   I. Title.

    PS3615.L439T56 2005   813'.6
                                    QBI05-800230

Synergy Books

10 9 8 7 6 5 4 3 2 1

The Time Has Come

The time has come for the wars of the world to end
The time has come for the rage and the hate to leave your hearts
The fighting will stop, the time has come, the time has come.
And the voices of the children will be heard
Heard around the world.
That was my intention, that was my plan
For the heart of a child to lead man.
The time has come for peace and love to reign.
The time has come to look in the eyes of each stranger you see
That stranger is me; you look at me, you look at me.
And the voices of the children will be heard
They'll be heard around the world.
That was my intention
That was my plan
For the heart of a child to lead man.

I have not abandoned you,
I am here to see you through
It was written from the start
You were meant to be a part of this moment,
And this moment is mine.

And the voices of the children will be heard,
Heard around the world.
That was the intention
That was the plan
Now the heart of a child will lead man.
The heart of a child will lead man.

This book is dedicated to John and Bethany and to all the children of the world who will teach us to live in peace.

The Time Has Come

I came to lead you to peace.

BRIDGEPORT, CONNECTICUT
JULY 22, 1999
2:33 AM

*T*he girl tried hard not to cry as she made her way up Bird Street in the direction of the Mary Immaculate Convent.

She walked past the darkened building, hoping against odds that a light would be on in one of the small windows on the second floor. If she could turn to anyone, it would be one of the nuns who ran the childcare center in the adjacent building. However, it was nearly 3 in the morning; no light shone in the window. She kept her head down and walked west on Worden Avenue toward the park.

She stopped when she heard a dog barking somewhere nearby, then a man's voice yelling obscenities to quiet it. She changed direction, heading away from the broken swings and damaged slide toward Bresco. The putrid smell from the waste management plant filled the air. Nearly there, she stopped abruptly as pain ripped through and around her middle. She grabbed for the wire fence that surrounded the place, the one that was supposed to keep people out.

Spotting an opening a few feet away, no doubt made by kids in the neighborhood, she pulled herself along until she pushed up the bent wire and went in.

When at last feeling safely concealed by the two large containers that were closest to the fence, she squatted down and leaned against one. Her lips parted, whispering words in prayer that nobody would see her and that the pain would go away.

She covered herself with thin arms in a feeble attempt to hide her body. Another sharp pain; she grabbed her belly which hardened under her touch. She gasped, sucking in as much air as she could, then began to pant in short choking sounds. Suddenly, the urgent need to relieve herself, followed by an urge to push, came over her; shame and humiliation quickly followed. Even in the worst of times, she had never soiled herself — except for the closet days. Sobbing uncontrollably now, tears pouring down her cheeks mixing with the sweat that dripped from her brow, she waited not knowing what would come next.

She pulled at the elastic waistband of the shorts hidden by a long tee shirt and pushed them down to her knees. Her stomach softened and the pain lifted. She glanced around and listened for sounds; nothing, she was alone.

The stench in the air added to her misery. Without pain for a moment, the child took in shallow breaths attempting to filter the foul odor from her lungs. On a good day, the smell made her sick to her stomach, now it was as though she was buried beneath the stench.

A wave of pain began gathering again in her back, then spread rapidly around to her middle. It came, hitting harder and faster than the last one. As her panic escalated, she sucked in as much air as she could in between sobs, not caring as to its source. The pain eased and the muscles around her middle softened again. She pushed her shorts completely off. She glanced up and saw a set of headlights coming toward her. Holding her breath and her belly, she lowered herself on to the ground, trying to become completely flat. It was impossible to do; she rolled over onto her back and lay still.

The approaching car did not slow down. She turned and tried to kneel upright, but stopped when suddenly caught in the middle of the move by another engulfing pain. However, this pain felt different, now there was a pressure between her legs that made her reach down and grab herself. She was on fire, she was splitting apart, the pain between her legs searing.

Her body began to shake; her sweat and tears melded, covering her now with a cold blanket of wetness. Liquid was pouring out from between her legs, she did not know from where and because of the dark she could not tell what it was.

She thought maybe it was blood but was afraid to imagine that she could bleed so much and not die. She placed her hand between her legs and felt a big, round, mushy thing pushing out of her. The panic she was already feeling began to swell; her heart raced, mounting, and matching rhythm to her rising fear.

She lay back down, on her side this time. Pulling her knees up to her chest as best she could, she began to bear down, determined to get this thing out. She was not going to let it kill her; not here on the roadside, in the dark of night with a rotten, dirty stench surrounding her.

Her belly hardened and the child pushed. Her body now engulfed with pain and fear and yet her determination to survive was stronger and so she bore down with every ounce of strength she had; she heard and felt a plop between her legs. She did not, could not, reach down there. This time, fear had won.

Her belly hardened again and she pushed once more. She grunted and pushed, feeling the thing between her legs moving out of her. Her crotch was splitting open, the pain ripped up her middle; she bit her lower lip so as not to let out a sound but lost the battle with an uncontrollable high-pitched wail. Then it was over. It was out.

She put her hands on her belly; it felt soft and sore, but much flatter than before. There was still a round pulsating bulge, but that other thing was out.

She heard a whimper and felt a fluttering movement between her legs. She stretched them out slowly. Her legs quivered from unfamiliar use; she kept them apart, careful not to touch the thing lying on the ground.

That awful thing had just ripped her body opened and caused her such pain. Her weakened state would not allow her to sit up without support of her hands resting on the ground behind her. Her fear was great, her curiosity even greater, forcing her look down in the direction of the sound. The whimpering and moving increased; the girl supported herself with one hand and reached the other forward toward the thing between her legs.

At the same moment, her belly tightened one more time and something else left her body. She pulled her hand back and felt her belly. It was not as flat as it had been, but it was not bulging anywhere else. She prayed again that all had left her.

Regaining her strength, she tried to sit upright just as another car, headlights glaring, came in her direction.

This time, however, she hoped the light would fall between her legs so she could see what she was hearing and feeling down there. The car passed and the ground in front of her became illuminated, but rather than reach down the girl put her hand to her mouth quickly to catch the gasp that involuntarily escaped.

Her mind raced, attempting to process what she was seeing. She pushed all thoughts and pictures away.

No. No. This was not real. There was nothing down there, nothing.

Images and sounds kept flashing in her mind but as quickly as they came, she pushed them out of her head.

She lifted her right leg up and rolled over onto her side and then onto her knees. Her head was swimming and her heart was ready to explode as saliva began to collect in the back of her throat.

She was on all fours now, rocking back and forth, the sweat building on her forehead and down her back once again; something else needed to come out of her small body, something causing even greater pain to the child.

She began to retch. Her head hung low and the sobbing and retching sounds that she could not contain cut through the dark's silence. When her moans softened and the retching lessened, the sounds continued to overshadow the soft whimpering from the small heap that lay next to her on the ground.

The girl gathered up her ache and began to force it out of her body, something she knew how to do quite well. Her rocking slowed to only a slight nodding of her head. She sat back, rested a hand on each knee and she looked upward. She gathered herself up by wrapping her arms around her aching body. Now silent, angry tears ran down her face. She let them fall.

Finally, she released herself. She sought and found her shorts and pulled them on. Roughly, she brushed away the tears on her face and her anger turned to rage. With new found strength, she pushed herself upright into a standing position, and raised her arms to the sky.

Making small fists with her hands, she shook them at a brilliant star that grew brighter by the second. She screamed words that only she could hear. She pounded her fists at the darkness; it did not matter that no one received the blows.

Another car approached, the headlights flickered in the distance. With fists still clenched, she lowered her arms, turned abruptly and exited the lot through the broken fence. She did not look back, but moved quickly and quietly away from Bresco; soon she was nearing her building in the P.T. Barnum Apartments.

A few early morning travelers passed unknowingly by the site, however, when the occasional glare of a headlight broke the dark, nothing was seen; only the sound of whimpering gave credence to the 13-year-old child who had come and gone alone into the night.

SWEET SPRINGS, MISSOURI
3 AM

*J*odie Sween sat up wide-eyed in his bed. At ten years old, there wasn't a night that he didn't sleep through; to say that this was an unusual event was a truth worth noting. Sleep was his respite from work.

Too much, work to do on the farm and not enough hands to do it.

His Pa said that about 50 times a day, or so it seemed. Now, here he sat, wide-eyed and awake not even knowing what time it was, but something made him stir — no, something made him more than stir in his sleep.

The urge to get up and awaken his twin brother Jason pushed him to lower his feet onto the wood floor and quickly walk the few steps to his single bed that was set in between the wall and window, the window facing north.

"JayJay" He whispered as he shook his brother. "Wake up, come on, wake up, something's— "

His bewildered other half opened his eyes, sat up and shuddered before the last of the words filled the air. There was no wind to be heard, or felt for that matter, but a cool current swirled around the small room.

Jason whispered back to his brother, "Come on, we gotta go."

The boys left their room, tiptoeing down the hallway to the front of the house. Jodie pushed open the screen door, and then eased the frame back into place so as not to let it bang shut.

They walked the hundred or so feet into the open area before the fields and stood still, planting their bare feet in the wet grass.

They kept their gaze upward. Neither spoke, they just stood there side by side, with arms touching and looking into the big dark sky of Missouri, which was decorated with a full moon and countless sparkling stars; their eyes fixed on the grandest one that was to the north.

It was a huge bright beam, boldly hanging in the sky; nothing else the two had ever seen came close to its splendor or majesty. The boys stared up at the brilliant star, then Jodie took hold of Jason's hand and both young heads tilted back, mouths fell open, each full of words that did not take sound.

Slowly, a beam radiating from the great star formed a white mist straight above their heads; it reached down and embraced them.

They stood in the center of it while light beams danced about them. There they stood with smiles on their faces and heads nodding in acknowledgment of what they were hearing and feeling. The white light that enveloped them began to lift and retrace its path to the star above; then it was gone. The boys stood side-by-side, hand in hand in the dark for a while longer before returning to their room.

They climbed into Jason's bed without speaking. Jodie closed his eyes then opened them quickly, "Hey Jay, you think we'll remember everything?"

In a sleepy state, his twin responded. "Yeah, when we need to, we'll remember all right. That was some star, huh?"

However, Jodie had already drifted back into a deep sleep, not waiting for the answer to the question — nor was Jason awake to hear the response.

Both boys slept peacefully for what was left of the night, with the words given by the star snuggled deeply into each young heart for safekeeping. However, had either boy stayed awake, he would have seen that the window in their room had nicely framed the great star that continued to glisten boldly throughout the night.

*T*he desert had put on her evening attire — dark, cool, and mysterious. The animals were making their sounds to let each other know of their existence. The crackle of the wood on the low-burning fire was the only noise made by the non-living. Every so often, there was a hiss, a punctuated crescendo in the fire's music.

A small hut, made of nature's goods, stood directly behind the fire. It had an odd shape, not square or triangular, nor rectangular, at best it could be called misshapen. It appeared ancient yet sturdy, seemingly unscathed by the wind or sandstorms that occurred regularly throughout the years in the region. How many years the hut existed, no one knew and exactly where it stood, no one knew that either.

A woman kept the dwelling. Absent of wrinkles the skin on her face was smooth, soft — the color of almonds. Her eyes were a light violet blue.

Her nose was straight and fit her face. She had white teeth and a full mouth made more prominent by high cheekbones. However, it was her hair that was her true distinction.

Her hair was golden. Not faded yellow or white like most old women, no, her hair was the color of gold and it flowed down her back, reaching her calves. When the wind blew, it would lift the woman's hair into the air, making a long trail behind her as though she were a shooting star and when set against the desert sky she appeared to be flying. There were tales reporting that on many dark nights she had actually appeared in the sky, her long golden hair flowing gracefully in the wind.

Stories such as this had become legends in the region, handed down through generations, fond stories to tell and to be heard by all.

No one from the nearby towns feared the talk of her; just the opposite, she sat high on the totem of honor. There were even some that prayed to her, calling her Gyada, Woman of the Wind. No one knew if that was her given name, however, she had been known as Gyada for as long as anyone could remember.

The story that passed from grandparents to parents to children was this: a young warrior, who later would become Chief, was out alone climbing high in the rocks, heading toward the caves to begin a vision quest.

Suddenly a great wind came up and swept him backward to the ledge below, crushing his back and knocking him unconsciousness. When he came to, a woman with long golden hair was kneeling at his side running her hands gently over his body from head to toe, chanting and lifting her eyes to the sky.

Then she placed her hands beneath him, lifting him ever so slightly off the ground. Her hands were hot and vibrating, all the while she chanted in a low tone. Suddenly, she removed her hands and placed one over his eyes, causing sleep to come over the man.

When he awoke, he was whole and no longer in pain, and the woman was sitting on a stone at his side looking at him. She stood, and extended her hand helping him up, smiled, then turned and began to walk away. The man called out to her to wait. When he asked her name, she responded in an unfamiliar language, one he could not hear with his ears; the woman spoke to his heart. Somehow, he understood all that was said but the only word that he could speak aloud was Gyada.

He called his thanks to her as she continued up the rocks. He watched in amazement, for it appeared that her feet did not touch the stone. Days later when he was returning to his village during the night, he looked into the sky and again to his bewilderment, there was the woman, with her golden hair flowing gently in the wind.

Of course, few, if any, people actually saw her over the years, but everyone knew the story and no one question nor doubted that it was true. The young warrior who later became Chief lived to be very old and now had been dead for well over a hundred years.

The fire continued to crackle outside the hut. The sky was still full of night but now a great star beamed in the north. Suddenly the woman in the hut stirred in her sleep. She opened her eyes and sat upright on her straw mat; words were forming in her mind then traveling to her heart, she smiled.

She is born. She came as promised.

The woman got up and wrapped a shawl around her shoulders. She lifted back the animal skin that was the door of her dwelling and entered the night. The fire gleamed up at her, extending a warm greeting.

Gyada picked up the stick that rested against the hut and gave her glowing friend a needed stir. She was still smiling from the words that had woken her from a sound sleep. She continued to stir the fire looking deeply into the embers. She lifted her eyes to the sky and embraced the star with love. Then she began her questions.

"What is her name?" She searched in her heart and remained, waiting for knowledge to come.

"They will know her as Grace."

"Grace? What will she do with such a name?"

The voice answered her, "She will teach them. They are in much need."

Gyada responded, "Are they ready?" No sound broke the night but still she heard.

"Some are, but many are not. But the time has come to fulfill the plan."

Gyada was full of questions. "How will a child be able to complete such a task?"

"It was so before time. Those chosen will learn from her knowing. It will take time, but she is the last of those meant to come, the last to be sent."

The woman put down the stick and glanced up to the sky. The dark was no longer in control of the night for the great star proclaiming the child's birth lit up the entire sky. Gyada lifted her arms into the air and began to chant. She chanted without movement or faltering in her rhythm for nearly an hour. When she was through, she lowered her arms and with one turn was back in the hut. She lay down on the mat and closed her eyes and with a smile across her face, she fell again into a deep sleep.

GROVER AVENUE
BRIDGEPORT, CONNECTICUT
4 AM

The alarm sounded loudly, signaling it was 4 AM. Albert's big black hand killed the sound with a single tap of a thick long finger. His wife Henna groaned, grabbed the pillow and placed her head beneath it to block out the sound, voicing her opinion of the alarm clock in muffled tones.

Albert slipped out of the bed quickly and headed for the bathroom to begin his morning ritual before going to work. Usually alert, he was tired this morning.

He did not remember being startled awake an hour earlier. He did not remember sitting upright nor shaking his head trying to rid himself of an unfamiliar feeling that grew inside his chest.

He did not remember opening his eyes wide and blinking repeatedly in an attempt to see something in the dark.

Then suddenly the feeling left him and he fell back and pulled the sheets around his shoulders, forced his eyes closed and drifted back to sleep. He didn't remember any of it as he made his way to the bathroom.

He looked into the mirror without much thought, running his hand over his face to feel the degree of roughness of his beard. He stifled a yawn, as he turned on the faucet to let the water run and heat up a bit.

He hated shaving in lukewarm water; it killed his face. The thought made him pat his cheek and smile at the vision of a baby's behind.

Damn, don't I wish I could be that smooth, he chuckled and ran his hand under the running water to see if it was hot enough.

Albert picked up his shaving mug and poured in some Black Magic Powder. He held the mug under the faucet and added just the right amount of water to make a thick lather. The shaving brush felt good in his hand.

He stirred it around slowly, thinking how long he had had that particular brush. *Let's see, Albert Jr. is nearly 34 and he gave it to me for Father's Day when he was eight.*

He whistled quietly at the number. *Twenty some-odd years — whew, that's a long time to hold the same thing in your hand every morning.*

Another smile crossed his lips. This time he thought of Henna. In a few weeks, they would be married for 38 years. He thought of holding her in his arms just about every night for the all those years.

What a woman.

He hooted aloud in spite of himself and in spite of the lecture that he knew he would get from her when he got home from work about being quiet in the morning.

He was blessed all right. He had himself a good woman to lie with at night and to laugh with in the daylight. On top of that, they had created three great kids that had produced six grandchildren with still more to come.

What more could a man ask for?

He finished shaving and leaned over the sink to wash off any remaining lather then grabbed the towel on the rack without looking and patted his face dry. He liked knowing where everything was without having to search. Like his wife and kids, he knew what to expect from them, most times.

Oh, Henna did surprise him on occasion, like when she announced she was going back to work last year. But he'd swallowed his words and said nothing. He just smiled broadly and asked when and where.

He had no complaints about Henna. She bore him children and raised them with manners, and morals and a sense of self-pride that no amount of outside influence could shake.

Albert remembered the time when Al, Jr., his only boy, had come home from school with a torn shirt and bloody lip.

He told them that a bully at school had taken his lunch and tried to beat him up as well. Al stood his ground and fought back, knocking the kid to the ground with his second swing. He then reached down and helped the boy up. He offered to share his lunch with him if the boy himself had none. This was how Henna and he had raised their children.

Oh, he knew he had been there as well, but a mother's love and firm hand is what shapes a child into an independent and strong adult. Albert felt his heart swell with pride and tears fill his eyes at the same time. My God, he had a lot to be thankful for.

Albert switched the light off and turned the doorknob quietly, returning into the bedroom to dress. He could see just as good in the dark as in the light. He contributed this to his waking and working in the very early morning hours for the last twenty-nine years.

He worked on the first shift at Sikorsky. He had worked himself up to be second in command of outdoor security and he really didn't have to be in at 5 AM anymore, but old habits are hard to break. Besides which, the day is still young when he left the plant, and that he liked just fine.

He liked driving to work in the breaking day, there was something special, almost holy, about the wee hours of the morning. Except for the smell near the entrance of 95, the new one near Bresco, the air smelled new and fresh each morning. And the birds in his neighborhood, he loved to hear the pretty chirps and whistles of the birds, breaking the quiet of the day that had yet to be intruded upon by noise of man.

If Albert had his way, he'd find a trick to keeping one whole day just like the early morning hours. Cool, with just a hint of light and it would be peaceful, real peaceful.

He would sip his coffee in the outdoor security booth, shooting the breeze with the night shift and watch as the sun began to peak over the horizon creating a purplish color in the sky. He had thought on more than one occasion that when his time came to pass on, this was the time of day to do it.

God surely must be keeping watch over His world during this holy moment and a man was sure to go straight to heaven if it was his time.

Albert walked into the kitchen, opened the refrigerator, reached in and took out the lunch that Henna had made for him the night before. He set the bag behind him on the counter without taking his head out of the fridge.

He reached for the orange juice and his other hand grabbed the carton of eggs. He lifted his foot to close the door, thought twice about the eggs, and put them back.

"*Too much cholesterol this week, gotta watch that these days.*"

He poured himself a tall glass of orange juice and drank it down in one long swallow. He put the carton back in the fridge, rinsed the glass, and placed it in the dishwasher, keeping in mind the things that Henna was particularly fussy about and dirty dishes and glasses in the sink were two of them.

He had to admit she was right; it only took a second more to open the dishwasher up and put things in. He walked quickly and quietly into the bedroom and laid his lips on Henna's warm cheek. He breathed in deeply and took enough of her scent with him to last the day. His hand slid tenderly down her back, he gave a loving pat then stood and moved away from the bed and out of the room.

As Albert opened the back door, he reached for his lunch and his car keys that hung on a hook nearby. He got into his car and began his drive to work. He entered the cool, dark morning with a smile on his face and a warm feeling in his heart.

~ ~ ~ ~ ~ ~ ~ ~ ~ ~

Albert backed out of his driveway and headed down Grover Avenue drinking in the sounds of the dark morning. He knew his route by heart and with little if any traffic on the road he was free to survey the sky longer than he really should while driving a car. The sun would not peek out of the horizon for a bit, but was hinting at it and a brilliant star blazed to the north. Albert thought to himself, funny, I never saw that one before.

He began his ritual of song. He started humming a hymn and then began singing the words from his soul in a deep bass voice holding the endnotes of each phrase with ease and solidity. His chest at times swelled with pride at hearing his own voice. Such vanity, but he knew the Lord, and was certain that Jesus, Himself, was smiling at the sound of hearing the gift He had bestowed.

He turned onto Brewster Street then took the right on Fairfield Avenue. The construction on 95 made his drive a bit longer these days, but he didn't really mind. He turned on to Wordin Ave, passed the Convent then onto Bostwick; he was heading to the new entrance ramp for the highway that was straight ahead about 100 yards or so.

He glanced at the clock on the dashboard: *4:30, right on the money. Darn, I forgot the pictures of the fishing trip. Teddy's gonna think I was lying for sure about that big old blue fish Al Jr. and I hooked onto last weekend.*

A smile crossed his face at the thought of his grandson Billy trying to lift that nearly 18-pound blue fish all by his sweet, five year-old self. Why, that bugger was nearly as long as he was tall.

Albert laughed aloud at the picture he had recaptured in his mind then returned to song.

I got joy, joy, joy, joy down in my heart, down in my heart. I got...

The familiar words were suddenly gone. He took his foot off the gas pedal, looked into the rear view mirror and pulled over to the side of the street.

He stopped the car. His eyes fixed on something in the middle of the road. It was not more than 10 feet in front of him. He blinked then blinked again. He could not clear up the white, cloudy haze that appeared before him obscuring all else in his line of vision.

His hands were on the steering wheel frozen in place. He was not afraid, just not sure of what he was seeing. He relaxed his grip on the wheel and placed his hands on his thighs, rubbing them back and forth, as though he was trying to get the feeling back in both. Albert sat there letting things settle in his mind and then in his heart. He was not ready to act, to make any kind of move so he sat, waiting on himself.

The image in front of him really had no definable shape and yet Albert could feel that it was in his likeness. He could not take his eyes away from the center of the translucent figure. He felt transfixed by it.

Keeping his eyes fixed ahead, he reached for the key in the ignition and turned off the engine. He felt the need to be closer to the light. Without thought, he placed his hand on the door handle and opened it slowly. Turning in the seat, he lowered his left foot to the ground, his right one was next as he simultaneously moved the rest of his body out of the car.

Albert stood with one arm resting on the top of the car and the other on the rim of the door. He stepped around the door and walked toward the white light. There was warmth flowing from the light making Albert feel as though he was being embraced by it. He walked the 10 feet or so to place him right in front of the glowing white presence.

Albert stood there with his arms hung down at either side of his body. No audible sound was heard, but he began to respond by nodding his head, "Yes."

In his mind, thoughts were rapidly entering, then traveling to and resting in his heart. He remained there, not moving a muscle, listening and answering without making a sound.

Tears began to roll down his face and his full lips began to turn upward, forming a smile. He lifted his arms with both his palms upward then he stretched his hands into the white light. He fell to his knees, looked up into light, and then closed his eyes.

The white light encircled him, embracing him, and for a moment, Albert became part of the light. Quickly, the moment passed and Albert opened his eyes to find that he was alone on the road. Time had stopped.

He was still kneeling with his arms stretched outward. He put them down slowly and stood up, glancing around at the same time. He stayed in this spot for only a few seconds and then he turned and began to walk to his right.

He followed the fencing that ran along the sidewalk. He looked up to see the billowing smoke stack of Bresco. He spotted an opening in the fence and crawled through. Albert stopped and turned his head to one side then the other, listening intently. Nothing, he heard nothing.

His eyes moved rapidly, surveying the space in front and to the sides of the huge containers facing. He listened again; both ears perked up. He shook his head, turning to the right he looked about; then he heard it – whimpering, soft whimpering. Albert moved forward slowly, scanning the area now with much purpose. The sound grew in his ears as he continued his search.

He walked as though on eggs shells. Suddenly, he stopped in his tracks. He took in a long and deep breath. His heart began to race as a sweat broke out on his forehead and down his back.

This cannot be happening, I must be dreaming.

Albert shook his head, trying to wake himself, beginning to fear this familiar yet strangely unnerving sound. A weakened cry came from the small bundle that lay in front of him. He got down on both knees about a foot away from the sound and stretched forward.

He tried desperately to adjust his mind, his heart, to what he was seeing and hearing. He reached forward and placed his large hand on the tiny little creature in front of him. It felt cold. Albert pulled his hand back quickly, frightened.

"Sweet Jesus, this is a live baby, my God, it's moving, and breathing."

Albert rested back on his the heels of his feet and again he rubbed his thighs back and forth in a nervous rhythm.

"This ain't gonna help no one. Get a hold of yourself man, come on now."

Albert began to take in deep breaths and count aloud. He got to five and the baby let out a strong loud wail as if to say get on with it.

"You're breathing and counting meanwhile I'm naked, cold and hungry."

Albert chuckled nervously, reached down, and with one swoop of his big hands picked up the tiny baby. He brought the infant close up to his face to look it over carefully.

A baby girl and a small one to boot. Albert guessed around five-and-a-half, maybe six pounds at best. He cradled her in his arms and eyed her from head to toe.

Her face was round and dainty. She had full lips and a narrow nose. She had stopped crying; her eyes were wide opened and looking directly at Albert.

They were light eyes. And although Albert knew that her vision should be blurry, he felt the infant was looking, knowingly, at him. Pretty, Albert thought to himself, the tiny baby girl smiled at him.

Albert's heart filled with emotion as he looked down at the baby in his arms. He lifted her gently and brought her close into his chest. He covered her body with his thick arms and began to rock her. Tears filled his eyes and ran down his cheeks on to the baby head. At the same moment, Albert felt the word Grace in his heart. He said the name aloud, smiling, liking the sound of it.

"Such a pretty baby you are, my sweet Grace."

His tears continued to fall on Grace's face. They began to roll into her mouth and she pursed her small lips trying to suck.

"Oh my, gosh, you must be starving! What the heck is wrong with me? "

Albert started to stand and realized the afterbirth was still attached to the umbilical cord. He lifted it gently and carried it with his other hand then hurried back to his car. He leaned in and popped the trunk opened, reached into the trunk and grabbed the blanket he kept in there for emergencies.

"This is one emergency I never thought of in my entire life."

He wrapped Grace in the blanket and set her next to him in the passenger's seat. He reached across her and pulled the seat belt around her trying to make her safe on the ride. He climbed into the driver's seat and sat placing his hands on his thighs again.

Drive.

"Where in God's name am I gonna go?" Albert looked down at Grace.

"First thing's first; she needs to get that cord cut. Susie's a nurse."

Susie was his second to oldest child. She worked in the emergency room of Bridgeport Hospital, but he knew she was at home at this hour.

"Maybe I should head there? No. Henna, Henna will know what to do."

At the moment of knowing where he was going, Albert started the car and began to drive. He drove with one hand and kept the other on Grace looking over at her every few seconds. He continued on the road until he could get off and head back in the direction of home. He thought briefly of the plant.

"Hell, I've got so much time off coming. I'll call in when I get home."

Albert drove with much more care than he had when he had started out this morning. He glanced at the clock: 4:45. Not even a half-hour had passed.

*That couldn't be, he thought, it feels like near eight hours since I stopped my car and was filled with...*Albert couldn't quite put a word on what he was filled with. It didn't matter though as he looked down at Grace and smiled broadly. He turned down his street anxious to present the child to Henna.

He pulled into the driveway and turned off the engine. Unbuckling his own seat belt, he turned to unfasten the one around Grace.

She was still awake. He took the keys out of the ignition and lifted her up with his right arm. He rested for a moment trying to think of the first words that he was going to say to Henna. He laughed out loud thinking of the expression; a picture is worth a thousand words.

Albert got out of the car and switched Grace into his left arm. He put the key into the hole and turned, he heard the dead bolt click. He removed the key, turned the doorknob, and walked into the kitchen quietly, but not quiet enough for a mother of three and grandmother of six.

"Albert? Is that you?" Henna voiced carried in from the bedroom. "What's wrong, you okay?" Henna had a concerned tone in her voice.

"Stay put, honey, I'm okay I just forgot something. I've got to call the plant. Stay in bed, I'll be right there."

He made a quick call to the plant saying he would be out today and maybe tomorrow, he'd call back later. He put the receiver back in the cradle. He looked down at Grace and smiled.

"Okay sweetie, now we face the music."

The bedroom lamp was off but the room was taking in light from the kitchen. Henna was on her side with her back to Albert and Grace. He tiptoed to her side of the bed and sat down. He leaned forward and kissed her hair. Henna smiled in her sleepy state and turned herself over. Without opening her eyes, she opened her arms to her husband, waiting for him to fill them up. She moaned slightly.

Albert felt himself stir at the sight of her. Amazed that after all these years this woman could make him come alive so quickly. He pushed that thought out of his mind and whispered her name.

"Good morning, honey."

He reached forward again kissing her gently but with passion on her mouth. He let his tongue move into her parted lips, running it over her smooth teeth. Henna reached her arms around her man and began to pull him toward her.

Albert ended the kiss, "Henna, wait." He sat up, breaking out of her arms.

Henna opened her eyes and looked into Albert's eyes. She saw a look she had never seen before. Then she looked down at what Albert was motioning her to look at. He was holding something in his arms, a bundle of sort. Henna was trying to focus her eyes in the dim light. She seemed unclear at what was in the blanket that Albert was holding so tenderly in his arms.

"Oh my God, Albert what is that? Is that? Oh my sweet Jesus, it's a baby. My God Albert, a baby. Where did you get it? Who does it belong to? Is it alive? Oh my sweet Jesus, a baby —"

Albert let Henna go on until he thought she could be still for a few minutes. He needed to try and explain the unbelievable event that had just happened without interruption.

"Henna, it is alive. And it's a baby girl. I found her by the road on my way to work."

That was it. That is all that came out of Albert's mouth. Nothing about the white light or the conversation, he had with the presence within. It was as though nothing else was going to come out of his mouth, so he closed it and sat there waiting for Henna to respond.

"You found her on the side of the road? Lying there, all alone? My God Albert, where is her mother? How could someone just leave a tiny little baby alone on the side of the road?"

Henna continued her litany of questions as she reached for Grace to look her over more closely. She let out a gasp she saw the umbilical cord and the afterbirth still connected to the child.

"Why she's just been born, Albert. She can't be more than a couple hours old. Who in their right mind could give birth to a precious thing like you and just leave you to die?"

Henna gathered up the naked baby and held her next to her face. The baby's tiny hand rested on Henna's mouth. She then shifted to a cradling position that prompted the tiny baby to seek out a source of food.

"Why, this poor child must be hungry."

For a moment, Henna wished she were still a young mother. Having breast-fed her own three, she would not have hesitated to let this baby nurse on her ample breasts.

"Albert, get me one of your undershirts." As Albert pulled a t-shirt from his dresser draw, Henna wondered aloud.

"This cord has to be cut and tied. Call Susie, tell her to come over. Don't say a word about the baby on the phone; just tell her to bring herself and her little black bag as quickly as she can."

Albert handed the undershirt to Henna who lifted the baby gently and put the shirt under her. "There now, that's softer than that old blanket isn't it sweetie.

"Bring me a nice warm, wet washcloth and dry hand towel so I can get this little honey cleaned up a bit. Then go to the store and get bottles and formula and water."

Albert was smiling. Thank God, he had this woman in his life. He did not mind one bit that she hadn't stopped ordering him around since she first picked Grace up.

Grace.

He forgot to tell Henna the child's name. Quietly he sat down next to Henna, handed her the warmed washcloth and towel and their eyes met.

Albert placed his hand on the child's head and spoke, "Henna, her name is Grace."

Henna put her own hand on the side of the baby's face and her fingers touched Albert's.

"Grace" She spoke the name softly and with much tenderness. Henna stroked Grace's face and then looked up at Albert. "Well, Grace is going to be sucking on air until you get to the store and back again. And don't you bother calling Susie I'll do it myself. It's more important for you to get formula and sweet water for this child."

As soon as Albert left the two females alone and went to the store Henna began to gently wash the newborn child. She surveyed her work and decided that it was good enough until the cord came off. She picked up the phone on the bedside table and dialed her daughter's number.

A sleepy voice answered. "Hello?"

"Honey, this is Mama, I need you to come over here, right now and Susie, come alone."

Susie woke up quickly. "Mama? What's the matter? Is something wrong? Are you or daddy hurt?"

Henna quickly changed her tone, realizing she must have scared her poor baby half to death.

"No, honey, your daddy and I are just fine. Honestly. But I do need your help. I can't go into it on the phone but if you could get James to mind the little ones, I really could use your medical knowledge."

"Mama, please, what's happened."

"Susie, this is your mother talking now. I am asking you to trust me and come here without me having to explain. You will hear, in fact you will see the entire story as soon as you arrive. Now drive safely, but hurry."

Henna hung up the phone without giving her daughter a chance to utter another word. Henna knew she could count on Susie. She looked down at the baby lying on her bed, "What in God's name are we going to do with you?"

She lifted the child in her arms and lay back on the bed. She lay there cradling Grace thinking back to the countless times she had held her own. There was nothing more precious than lying in bed with a child snuggled in your arms.

Nothing except when Albert was there as well. It was special whenever the children joined them in bed, as a new child or an older one in need of loving and comfort. Many a cherished memory was shaped recalling when all three of the children climbed in between the two of them for one of Albert's bedtime stories that was told with much enthusiasm.

She thought of her life thus far; it was full of many blessings, joys and much love. She let the latter pour out of her at this moment and embraced the child that lay in her arms. Henna thought of how she came into the world; left alone on the side of the road. She thought of the young woman who gave birth to this beautiful baby.

Her eyes filled with tears and her heart with sorrow. What pain had caused that woman to abandon her baby in such a way? Henna wished that for a moment the mother of this child were also here in her bedroom. She wished that she could put her arms around her and offer comfort for surely it was needed.

She knew the pain of giving birth with no baby to show for it. Henna's thoughts traveled back in time to when she was barely 15, she had been raped and a pregnancy had resulted.

Everyone thought it best if she gave up the child; her parents made the decision for her. She never even got to hold it or even lay eyes on it, never knew if she had a boy or girl. They took her baby as soon as she gave birth and gave it away. She woke up the following morning with an ache in her heart the size of a mountain.

It took a long time for that ache to leave her. If she were honest, she would admit that the pain had never completely gone. This morning was the first time in a long time that she had allowed herself to feel her loss again. Henna wiped away the tears and smiled down at Grace.

"I won't abandon you, honey, not on my life."

~~~~~~~~~

Albert hurried out of the supermarket with two bags of baby things. While there, he saw other things that Grace would need.

Diapers and powder, little tiny tee shirts, lotion and Q-tips; he didn't remember exactly why but he remembered Henna using lots of Q-tips when the kids were little. He also found a small stuffed doll and rattle. The whole purchase came to nearly forty dollars.

"My God, babies have gotten awfully expensive."

He thought aloud at the register. The cashier gave him a funny look; Albert realized he must have looked kind of strange.

After all, it was not even six in the morning and here was this old guy buying all this baby stuff.

"My grandbaby is coming today and I thought I might just stock up on things, case my daughter runs out."

Albert did not say another word. He paid the cashier, picked up his bags and hurried to the car. When he pulled into the driveway Susie's car was parked out front of the house. Albert wondered how she was taking to Grace.

He came in the back door for the second time that morning. He set the bags of baby supplies down gently on the counter listening for sounds from the bedroom.

He heard whispering but could not make out words. He thought about his daughter, Susie. He smiled. She was a beautiful woman.

She resembled Henna at her age; his little baby girl was a grown woman of thirty-two. She had two children of her own that she was raising with the same set of values and love that she was given. A parent could not be more proud then when a child willingly passes on what has been taught.

And she was bright. Susie had graduated top in her class from nursing school and had been the only one of her class allowed to begin her nursing career in the busy emergency room. She worked full-time till the kids came along then went back to a career that she loved part-time. Henna and Albert helped her out with minding the kids on the days she worked. They enjoyed themselves as much as the grandbabies did on those days.

Albert left his thoughts and the bags in the kitchen and walked into the bedroom. No one was there. He followed the sound of the voices to the bathroom. He could see Grace lying on the counter, Henna had hold of her little arms and legs real gentle like while Susie was busy cutting the cord and clamping it off.

Working the emergency room all these years had given Susie quite a supply of unusual medical equipment. On more than one occasion, she had left work with a disposable suture kit in her green scrub's pocket. She tossed them on the dresser with the other countless pens and notes, as she'd undress before her shower after a long and exhausting workday.

Usually she would bring them back to work but with two kids and four nieces and nephews, she figured it wouldn't be such a bad idea to keep one or two around, so she added them to her own black bag. The *just in case* one that she took on outings and vacations; this was the bag that Henna had asked her to bring along on this early morning visit.

"There, that should do it."

Susie straightened up and surveyed her worked. The cord was now clamped and cut about an inch from Grace's belly. There was no drainage from the cord and Grace looked like any other new born. Susie smiled down at the little baby and her work. She reached down and picked up Grace.

She cradled her in her arms, "That's better, isn't it, sweetie."

Grace moved her arms about and her tiny hand touched Susie's face. She held it there for the briefest moment. Suddenly a faint tinkling sound broke the silence in the room. All three grown-ups began to laugh as the Grace peed on the floor. Albert laughed the loudest.

"Not to worry, Henna I got a box of disposable diapers with the rest of things you asked for."

"That's a good thing, because I was just about to use one of your tee shirts to cover this little bottom." She patted Grace's tiny little rear end and then took her little hand in her own two.

"Wouldn't you just love to wear Albert's shirt, Grace?"

Susie handed the baby over to her mother and cleaned up the mess as she spoke to her parents.

"So Daddy, Mama said you found this baby by the side of the road. Exactly where and how did you spot such a tiny little thing? And where's the mother? Didn't you see anyone around that could possibly be the mother? Most women don't just give birth by the road side and get up and walk away."

Albert was trying to speak but his daughter kept going on, one more of her likenesses of Henna. She began to ask questions that he couldn't answer. All he could remember about this morning was being out of his car and on the embankment. There was something else but it was fuzzy.

It had been clearer when he had first come home this morning, but now he was not quite sure what had happened. The only thing he was sure about was the reality of this baby. He felt something in his heart for her the minute he picked her up. He knew that he was meant to find her.

Deep in his soul, he felt a stirring that gave him comfort. It gave him a sense of knowing about what he was to do with Grace. He was not going to question it he was just going to accept it.

Everyone had moved into the kitchen where Susie began to make a pot of coffee and Albert unloaded the bags. He opened the box of diapers and handed one to Henna.

"Daddy, are you listening to me? You look as though you're in a trance."

"No, no, darlin' it's just I'm waiting my turn, waiting until you've finished, but look at these? Aren't these the tiniest things you've ever seen?" He held up one of the newborn diapers that were smaller than his own hand.

"Daddy, you forget that my Jillian is only two years old. It wasn't so long ago that she was wearing that size. Now she brings me her own to change, and you'll be happy to know she is just about to be potty trained."

Henna reached for the diaper and spoke to Grace, "Don't worry baby, while these two are yapping away I'll put some clothes on you and get some food in your hungry little tummy."

She had already found the package of undershirts, opened them and began putting one on Grace. She continued to join in the conversation.

"Honey there's some fresh coffee cake sitting under the cake tin if you'd like."

"No thanks, Mama. Daddy, you want me to cut you a little piece? How about you Mama?"

Albert had already reached for a plate answering Susie's question.

"Maybe after I feed Grace, and Albert before you begin feeding your own face, would you mind opening one of those little bottles of sugar water and handing it to me?"

Doing as told Albert pulled one of the small bottles, twisted the cap and turned the inverted nipple right side up, tightened it just so and handed it to Henna. Grace accepted the nipple hungrily into her tiny mouth and began to suck looking like any other newborn feeding for the first time. Albert sat down at the kitchen table and picked up his fork getting ready to sink it into the piece of coffeecake that sat in front of him.

"Daddy I'm waiting for some answers. Tell me about the baby."

"I guess I'll never taste this cake with you two women around."

He set his fork down and began to speak. He didn't know what would come out of his mouth so he let the words wander out on their own.

"Like your Mama told you, I found her on the side of the road on my way to work. I didn't see anyone around. Or hear anybody for that matter. The only thing I heard was the sound of this little one crying. I only stopped my car 'cause I thought I saw something in the road.

"I guess I thought it was a hurt animal or something. When I got out, that's when I heard Grace. I looked around and then I spotted her — good thing, too. She was cold when I first picked her up, and wouldn't have lasted much longer by the looks of things."

Albert paused for a moment and took a bite of cake and a gulp of coffee. "I held her in my arms, after birth and all, and figured I had to do something quick. So, I thought of you, Susie.

He continued. "I thought you could help with cutting her cord and Henna could help by, by, he smiled at his wife, by just being Henna. And look, I was right about both. You fixed Grace up just the way it's done in the hospital. And look at your Mama honey, there isn't a better person on the face of the earth to love and nurture a child."

"But Daddy, why didn't you take the baby to the hospital? What made you bring her home? Don't you think it would have been wiser to take her to the emergency room? What if something had gone wrong? What if the baby had died? What if someone is looking for her and what about the mother? Maybe she's at the hospital right now."

Albert raised his finger to his lips to silence his daughter.

"First, let me say I really don't know why I did what I did. I acted from my heart, Susie not with my mind. When I lifted that baby into my arms I felt as though she trusted me to do what I thought best, and I do believe that so far I have done just that.

"Second, about her mother - there was no mother around. I did look around at first and there was not one living soul 'cept for Grace to be seen or heard. This child was out there alone, and chilled to the bone. I was not going to take time to look for the person who left her there. I had to concern myself with the baby. She came first, nobody else."

While Albert caught his breath and took another bite of cake, Henna added her own thoughts.

"The mother must have been a child herself, or at the least very disturbed. No reasonable woman would just give birth and leave their baby alone in the middle of the night, on the side of the road.

"Think about it, Susie. She must have been pretty upset and scared to do such a thing. Maybe she was hiding and watching and when she saw your father rescue her baby, she felt it was okay. I don't know for sure, I'm just thinking out loud. I kind of wish your Daddy found the girl who felt so alone in the world that she left her baby; I wish he had brought her home too. She must be one sad and aching creature right this moment."

Grace was on Henna's shoulder now. Henna gently patted her tiny back trying to encourage a healthy burp. She made small circles with her hand and began a rhythm with her beats.

Finally, Grace let out a burp.

"That's my baby, doesn't that feel better now?" Henna spoke to the child as though she was one of her own.

"Mama, listen to you. You and Daddy act as though you are going to keep this child. You can't. You can't possibly keep this baby. What in God's name, are you going to do with her? And someone must be looking for her even if you're right about the mother. Someone must have known about this baby. The fact that the girl was pregnant —"

Susie stopped her verbal onslaught abruptly as she was taken back to her work in the emergency room. She knew it was quite possible to be nearly full-term and still be able to conceal it from everyone.

Just last month a 14-year-old had arrived at the ER doubled over with abdominal pain. She had no idea that she was seven-and-a-half months pregnant, fully dilated, and ready to deliver.

When the staff tried to explain what was going on, why she was in such pain she freaked out. So did her mother who had brought her in. Neither the girl nor her mother had known she was pregnant and neither was prepared or able to handle the situation.

The mother began to hit the girl right there in front of everyone. She slapped her repeatedly calling her a whore and slut. There was no mercy or compassion from mother to child, only rage. The staff had to pull her away from the girl who was now in a state of shock.

The mother left, screaming angry words at her 14-year-old girl, "Bitch, you can sleep on the streets for all I care! Don't think you're coming back to my house with your stinking bastard brat. I got enough problems without having you around and another kid to feed."

With that, she stormed out of the hospital. She hadn't given any information to the clerk yet, so nobody knew what her last name was or how to reach her, for that matter. Social Services could press charges of neglect since the girl was only 14 but they would have to find this woman first.

When the young girl began to slip into clinical shock, an alert ER staffer quickly started an I.V. and placed her on oxygen.

Soon she started to come around a bit, emitting a low wail that sent chills up the spines of the medical workers.

No one could comfort her. She took hold of the side rails, looked up at the ceiling, and howled. A nurse hooked her up to a fetal monitor and could see that the baby was in distress and her labor was full blown.

The contractions were coming close and hard and yet she didn't seem to be reacting to them but more to the horror of being alone; she remained fixed in one position. The OB team leader spoke, "We'd better get her into delivery... she's more than ready."

The team raced with the girl's stretcher through the halls. When they reached their destination and tried to lift her onto the table, she would not let go of the railings.

As Susie spoke quietly and calmly to the young girl, she tried to pry her hands free. Suddenly the girl stopped wailing. Her already pale skin blanched, the sheet around her began turning a deep shade of blood red.

Before the entire staff, the child began to hemorrhage; then she arrested.

"*Code Blue Delivery Room. Code Blue Delivery Room.*"

The message spread quickly throughout the entire hospital via the Intercom System. The team lifted her onto the delivery table now without the resistance and began CPR.

"She's not responding. Give me another amp of Lidocaine. Shit. Nothing. Goddamn it, come on girl! Live! Let's go, start pumping your heart."

"Clear!"

The girl's body jolted from the shock of electricity that was zapped through her body. Nothing. The Team Leader ordered, "Again, up it five. Step away."

Still no response. The girl's heart refused to take back the rhythm that had sustained life only moments before.

"The baby is in distress, I gotta get it out now." The OB looked into the eyes of the lead medical person.

"I'm not giving up on her. Can you take the kid out in less than three minutes? "

"I can't do better than that and still not be in your way."

"Then do it — now."

The OB team swarmed the table, leaving only the upper half of the girl to the other team. ER staff continued to bag the girl and rotate the task of chest compression while the OB team focused on the unborn child who was struggling to stay alive in his mother's lifeless body.

The OB resident spoke.

"Are we ready? Okay, kid, it's your turn. Let's go."

Within seconds she had cut across the girl's abdomen, two "assists" were clamping of the bleeders as the resident made a thin incision into the uterus.

"There's the baby. Is the NIC hot box ready?"

"Ready and waiting."

She made the cut, then handed the scalpel to the scrub nurse and reached in and pulled out a blue skinny rag doll that was supposed to be a baby.

It was a boy. She lifted it quickly and one of the assists reached in for the placenta. It had separated from the uterine wall. They clamped the cord off in two places and cut it. The doctor handed the infant over to the third team that had quickly gathered to work their magic.

The medical doctor yelled, "Open her up all the way — stop the bleeding. If we're going to save this kid, we gotta stop the bleeding and get her heart pumping. I want to do an open massage."

Within seconds, the girl's entire midsection was open, her sternum lifted and separated, and the pericardium sac sliced carefully to reveal her lifeless heart. The doctor reached in, took her heart in his hand, and began squeezing.

"Come on, baby, beat for Papa." He kept on massaging until his hands were aching, then someone else relieved him. Still the girl did not respond. They continued to work to bring life to the girl.

A third person on the team took their turn on massaging the heart, still no spontaneous cardiac activity.

"Time?"

"Thirty-seven minutes." Thirty-seven minutes had passed since CPR had begun. The head of the team spoke.

"That's it, folks. There's nothing else we can do. We tried. This kid just doesn't want to play ball with us. I'm calling it."

He tried to bring a halfhearted degree of lightness to the end of a grim situation. The team member who held the lifeless heart in her hands continued rhythmically squeezing away, reluctant to give up.

"She only a kid, Pat. I have a niece this age, I can't just give up on her."

"Micki, you haven't given up, I'm calling the shots, its okay. You can stop now."

He placed his hand on hers while it was still squeezing the heart of the 14-year-old on the table. Pat gently pulled Micki's hands out of the girl's chest cavity. He took her hands in his own and looked into eyes brimmed with tears.

"We did the best we could possibly do. She didn't want to come back and by the way things went in ER, it sounds like she didn't have too much to come back to."

Micki leaned her head on his chest.

"She was a baby; a baby having a baby. What's wrong with our world that children have babies? That they don't even know that they're pregnant and the mothers are throwing their kids out at a time when they need them more than ever. Part of me understands why this girl didn't want to live, and another part is so angry with her that I want to scream. How does this happen in this day and age?"

"Micki, I can't begin to explain the God-awful state that our world is in, all I can do is try and patch it up when it enters through the doors of the ER."

The two separated and watched as the other team members disconnected tubes from the girl's body. Pat removed the retractor that had separated the sternum.

He left the other clamps in place knowing that the girl would continue to bleed, it was still too soon after her death. She would be in more of a mess when she hit the morgue, so it was only right to give her some dignity.

He pushed the section of her midsection together and without asking, was handed a long, wide strip of tape to stick across it. Micki handed him another until there were three pieces of tape holding the girl's body closed.

Susie, who had been part of the medical team, lifted a warmed sheet from the container nearby. These sheets were kept close by for the mothers in labor who often went from being very hot to very cold.

She didn't know why she was covering the dead girl with a warmed sheet but it seemed the thing to do. With the top of her arm she brushed away her own tears. It was about the only part that was not splattered with the girl's blood. Susie covered the girl's body slowly, hesitating when she got to her head.

She looked at the face of this young girl. The remains of a recent beating were still evident; there was a yellowing beneath the left eye and a cut over the brow. The rest of her features were not notable. They hadn't quite taken on a woman's appearance. How sad that her body had been plunged in headfirst into this thing called womanhood.

Susie could not bring herself to cover the child's face. It happened too quickly, she should be planning her first year at high school. She should be worrying about how to fix her hair and what color nail polish is in. Micki stood by Susie's side and gently pulled the sheet up over the girl's face. She placed her arm around Susie.

"You okay?"

"No, I'm not, but I will be. I don't ever want to get so hardened by all this madness that I don't feel sadness or anger."

"I know what you mean. It's all so senseless."

"Excuse me, ladies, I have to bring her downstairs, the ER is calling for both of you."

The orderly lifted the girl without help unto the stretcher that would end up at the morgue. He placed the heavy plastic covering over the railings to disguise the death chariot as it was wheeled through the corridors of the hospital. The orderly pushed the stretcher without much thought or effort through the electric doors and vanished as he turned the corner.

Susie and Micki's thoughts both turned at once to the baby that had just been born. "What do you think? Is there a chance for the kid?

Micki spoke without thinking. "Maybe, but if he's going to make it he'll make it here. They've got the best staff and equipment around. He didn't look too good; I only got a real quick peek at him. God, he was so blue."

The rag-doll blue baby did not make it. By the time Susie returned to the ER and began the paper work on the dead girl, Pat came strolling over with his head lowered.

"The kid never even took a breath. They worked on him for a half an hour. Nothing. Nada. The only thing good about this whole situation is I know he met his Mama and she carried him to heaven with her."

His eyes remained dry but his tone was somber, he turned quickly before Susie could ask any questions.

Susie stared at the papers in front of her. She had nothing but the girl's first name - Missy. The girl had said nothing when asked, but the mother had used the name Missy. She had screamed it at her with such anger. There was no love attached to the name; it could have been a euphemism for all that matter.

Maybe she'll calm down and come back. Maybe she'll be sad over the deaths of her child and grandchild. Susie did not put much hope in that happening; it was just two less mouths to feed for the angry woman who stormed out of the hospital.

Susie came back to the present. She looked at her parents; both sets of eyes were on this baby girl, they lovingly called Grace.

What right did she have to tell them what they should and should not do? What right did she have to send this baby out into an unknown and possibly loveless world — she'd probably end up back up on the side of the road, one way or another.

Here, this baby would get all the things that her parents had given her. Protection, food, clothing, a great deal of joy, and most importantly love. In her heart, Susie knew she could not deny this baby her parent's presence.

She walked over quietly and stood over her mother's shoulder.

"Hello, Grace, welcome to the family." She stroked the baby's head, liking the feeling of her soft black hair.

Albert looked at his daughter, his eyes filled with tears as he watched her stroke Grace's head, which was resting sleepily on Henna's shoulder, and one more time that morning he counted himself a lucky man. He knew that God was indeed watching closely over his family.

CIBOLA, NEW MEXICO

*T*he sun was at mid-peak and Gyada had been up for several hours. She walked along the caves on the south side of the valley then entered the cave to the left of a huge mountain. The mountain had a long cool stream that flowed from the top down the side where Gyada now stood. Inside the cave, a tributary emptied into a deep pool of water. The water was not ice cold, as one would expect, but hot, soothingly hot.

Steam came up from the large pool and a mist covered most pathways. This was one reason that no one but a foolish man would enter this dwelling alone, no one except Gyada. She knew this cave as well as she knew the sky.

Gyada moved forward in the cave with confidence, holding her walking stick as one would hold the hand of a companion. She passed by the pool of water and stood facing it for a moment. She spoke quietly in tongue, then lowered her head in deference, and then moved on. She passed under the waterfall that filled the pool. She entered the belly of the cave. The passage was dark but Gyada knew and saw her way without faltering.

There was a light shining ahead. Gyada, paused, smiling to herself she began to chant in a low tone. She reached the lighted area of the cave. The illumination was coming from an opening in the ceiling of the cave that was nearly 60 feet above her. It was wide enough to let in enough light to make the area seem like early morning.

Gyada stood in the center of the light. She set her walking stick on the ground next to her. She raised both her arms over her head and began to chant. There was an echo in the chamber giving her words even more purpose. She stopped and sat down on the ground, where she stood.

She spoke in her own words. She spoke without sound.

"Where is she now? When will she be able to hear my words? When will our hearts have the same rhythm, our breath become one breath?"

Gyada waited but soon her heart became full with the responses.

"She is where she was sent. Be patient, woman."

Gyada seemed anxious, "How much longer shall I stay?"

"Until it is time, but you must be mindful, for she will call to you in the night. She will whisper your name. You must listen for her. Listen. Soon she will whisper your name softly."

"What should I say to this child?"

"Speak from your heart Gyada; speak through your spirit who places the words within you. You will say only what you know to be truth. Speak with purpose and guidance. She will ask many questions but will know more than she asks."

Gyada sat there in the belly of the cave for a long time. She let the thoughts weave in and around, and through her. Her heart was full and for the time, she felt satisfied. She waited until the light from the ceiling was gone. She lay down, closed her eyes, and then fell into a deep sleep.

When the child is born
her mother is the moon,
her father the sun.
The trees and birds her
brothers and sisters;
The wind her breath of life;
She is without color
or creed, hate
or fear.
She is truth.

The Family

Grace was perched in an infant seat in the middle of the kitchen table. She kicked the soles of her feet against the padding and waved her arms about to the music of Albert and Hennas' voices. The two of them sang and moved about the kitchen preparing for the dinner they were having with all the kids that night.

They sang familiar words to an old song, "*Someone's in the kitchen with Dinah, someone's in the kitchen I know oh, oh someone's in the kitchen with Dinah strumming' on the old banjo.*"

Albert sang and set out the dishes on the table around the infant seat. Grace was laughing and moving her arms faster and faster.

"Looks to me as if she wants to dance, Albert." Henna saw the glee on Grace's little face.

Not needing any more prompting than that, Albert unbuckled the safety belt around Grace and swooped her up in his arms. He lifted her up into the air and swung her around as Henna clapped and continued the song. On that last long note, Albert gathered Grace into his arms and smothered her belly with "raspberries" causing her to squeal with delight.

He brought her close to his face, looked into her eyes, kissed each soft round cheek, and then laid his own, shaved baby smooth, next to hers. He whispered in her tiny ear, "I love you, baby."

Henna's eyes misted over at the sight of her man and child. She joined them and put her arms around Albert. She rested her head on Grace's small back. "I love you too, sweetie."

The three of them stayed in the center of the floor swaying, ever so gently, to the music that hung in the air. Henna glanced up at the clock.

"Sweet Jesus, the kids will start piling through the door any minute. The chicken is not even on the table. Enough playing you two, we have work to do. "

"Albert, go put Grace's little pink outfit on her; the one I set on our bed. Ruthie picked that up at the mall the other day. She thought that Grace would look pretty in it. I think Ruthie is just tired of buying for her three boys. It is such fun for a woman to shop for a baby girl."

Henna kept talking as Albert meandered into the bedroom and lay Grace on the bed. She only had on a terry jump suit with snaps that he effortlessly pulled apart. He sniffed.

"Looks like you need a changing, sweet Grace."

He smiled down at her. "How come it seems like you're always messy when I change you? I swear honey, you could save a poop or two for your Mama; she loves a messy diaper."

Grace looked up at Albert and reached her hands toward his face. Albert finished wiping, swiping and diapering as he liked to put it, and lowered his face to Grace's out stretched arms. Grace put her two hands on either side of Albert's big soft face. She patted his cheeks and looked into his eyes. Albert could not help but plant a kiss on the tip of her little nose.

"Okay, we best be moving along here kiddo, Henna's going to be calling us to task for playing on the job."

As Albert turned Grace over, to button the tiny little button on the back of dress Henna called from the other room.

"Here they come."

The sound of the back door opened and Susie and her brood came rushing in. Her husband, James, carried Jillian on his shoulders, requiring him to duck as he entered the kitchen.

"Put her down before you decapitate her, James." Susie sounded just like Henna, bossy but loving.

"Billy, did you bring in the other bag like I asked?"

Five-year-old Billy, his arms laden down and his face completely hidden, by a huge white garbage bag, shouted from behind, "Mama, who do you think is carrying this, Santa Claus?"

"That's enough out of you smarty pants."

Both Susie and Henna were having a hard time suppressing their laughter.

"I found a whole bunch of Jillian's baby clothes for Grace up in the attic. Some might be too big right now, but I don't have to tell you Mama, how quickly a baby grows. They're all clean and ready to put away. When Ruthie comes the three of us can sort though and put away what will fit her now. The rest, well, you have more storage room than I do Mama, it's all yours."

As Susie finished her sentence, Ruth, her husband Peter and their three sons, Pete Jr., Samuel and Michael came through the kitchen door. Peter let out a howl,

"Ooooh, what's smells so good? Mama's been cooking all day for sure, Ruthie honey, how about taking a few more cooking lessons from Mama, I'm sure she wouldn't mind. Especially if she knew what last night's dinner tasted like."

Ruthie gave her husband a playful jab in the stomach, which made all three little boys jump on their father.

"You know a woman can't be everything, Peter. I might not cook like Mama but I sure as hell can love like her and now you tell me what's more important? Right Mama?"

Albert and Henna had never been shy around the children when it came to displaying how much they loved one another.

One of Albert's pet phrases was, "Jeez Louise, that woman still makes my hair stand on edge." Their children loved how much they loved one another. The loving trickled down from parents to children, who knew the importance of a healthy, loving marriage. The kitchen was full of laughter and raucous remarks when Albert, Jr., his wife Betty and nine-year-old daughter Elizabeth walked in.

"Hey, everybody," Al, Jr. gave Henna a kiss on her extended cheek. "How's one of my three favorite women?"

Betty set a chocolate cake down on the counter and spun around to her mother-in-law.

"Well, if I'm one of those three I sure wouldn't mind a little extra attention these days." Her belly was swollen with child. Her due date was still more than two months away and the warm late September days were getting to her.

"Mommy, let Grammy feel the baby kick."

Elizabeth pulled Henna's hand toward Betty's bulging middle and held it there until all three smiled at the slight kick that was felt by them all.

"It's a boy, Henna. I just know it's a boy. Not that I would mind another sweet girl like my baby."

Betty held Elizabeth's face in her hands and smiled at her little girl.

"But a boy would be nice this time."

Ruthie piped up, "Oh, really? You should try living with four of them. I can't remember the last time I went to sit on the toilet and didn't have to put the seat down. And don't get me started on weekend sports. All blessed day, Betty, all blessed day. I'm thinking of moving back home."

Peter and four-year-old twins, Peter Jr. and Samuel, and three-year-old Michael all began to wail.

"Ooooh, Mama doesn't love us any more."

"Oh, hush, you guys, you know I love you all to pieces. But just once, I would like to get up in the middle of the night and not fall into the toilet."

Unnoticed, Albert stood holding Grace in the doorway of the kitchen, watching his brood. He was responsible for all that filled his house this day.

What more could a man want in life? He could never figure that out. He was happy. More than happy — most times he was overjoyed.

He held Grace up close to his face. Her head rested on his chin. She, too, was taking in the room filled with love and laughter, as though she knew had become a part of it.

Suddenly, as if rehearsed, the room became quiet and everyone turned to look at Albert and Grace. "Hello, Daddy, and how's my precious Grace?"

Ruthie planted a kiss on her father's cheek and reached for Grace at the same time. "My goodness, how much have you gained since last week, you little piggy wiggly? Mama, what are you feeding this child? Surely, she must be close to 15 pounds."

Henna patted Grace's bottom but left here in Ruthie's arms.

"Why, just three days ago at the doctor's, she tipped the scale at 14 pounds, seven ounces. She's eating like your father, Ruthie, in fact keep an eye on those chicken legs tonight, she just might jaw on one.

Isn't that right baby?" Henna kissed Grace's little foot, which was covered with a tiny ruffled sock.

"Okay, when are we eating, woman? My stomach is crying out loud from hunger. Poor Grace is getting worried I might fade away."

Albert made a sorrowful noise and all the grandchildren attached him playfully.

"Help me, somebody, I got all these sea monsters on me. Henna, save me, sweet darlin'."

"Albert, you can save yourself, I'm going to start serving dinner."

Everyone pitched in to ready the tables for the meal. Grown-ups sat in the dining room and the kids sat in the kitchen, but since only a doorway separated the tables, it felt as though everyone was eating together.

Albert set Grace in her swing and gave the handle a few turns. He gently pushed the swing forward and the rhythm began. Grace sat contentedly sucking on her little fist and making a swipe every so often at the soft pink stuffed ball that Henna had tied to the front of the swing.

"Let us bow our heads and give the Lord thanks, everyone."

Albert led the prayer as his family joined hands.

"God, you have blessed this family with your ever present love. We are thankful and hopeful that you will continue to be part of our lives each and every day we live. We will continue to share with our brothers and sisters as you have taught us. We thank you for our bounties and trust that you will watch over us and the world in which we live. And God, thank you, thank you for our Grace. Amen."

In unison, Albert's family joined in a resounding "Amen! Now let's eat!"

The litany around the table began.

"Pass the peas James, please."

"Mama, do you want a roll?"

"Hey, Peter, leave a little chicken for the other end of the table will ya."

"Ruthie, this salad is moving on do you want some or not?"

The children's table was no different. Their voices mixed and mingled one after another equally heard, contributing to the typical dinner chatter. The tables exchanged conversation at will.

"Granddaddy, did you eat that fish we caught yet?"

Billy had told his friends at school about the size of the blue fish. Elizabeth piped up from the children's table.

"Is Grace still awake, Grammy?" she asked, anxious to hold Grace, knowing it was good practice for the new baby soon to be born into her own family.

"She's still wide awake. Swinging and singing. She loves that thing. Thank God you saved all your baby things from Jillian, Susie. They came in handy unexpectedly."

Henna smiled across the table at Albert, and then leaned over to pat Grace's cheek. She gave the swing handle a few more turns, continuing its back-and-forth rocking motion.

James spoke, directing his question at Albert.

"Has there been any word? I mean, is anyone asking you anything about Grace?"

Albert paused a moment then answered his son-in law.

"No, James, not one single question, not one word. It was like no one cared or knew about anything. This child just appeared before me and here she is as living proof.

"We listen to the news every night, don't we Henna, and we have yet to hear one word about a newborn baby missing or young mother admitted to a hospital. It's kinda like she just dropped out of the sky. It's like a miracle, James. No, it *is* a miracle."

Al Jr. added his two cents, "It would seem to me that someone had to know that this girl was pregnant, or see something."

Susie, remembering otherwise, responded for her father.

"That's not necessarily so, Al. I've seen it more than once in the emergency room when a girl or even a grown woman comes in not even aware that she is in full blown labor, let alone pregnant."

"But Susie, what do you think happened to the mother? I mean, could someone just deliver this baby on the side of the road, get up and walk away and just go on about her life, like nothing even happened?"

"My dear brother, I can't begin to speak for another woman, but I know that the mind is capable of blocking and or shutting down when it needs to or wants to. More than likely, that is exactly what happened. Of course, I can't say for certain. I'm just glad it was Daddy who found Grace and not someone else."

"Look, Mama, she's asleep. You want me to put in her crib?"

"That's okay, Betty, leave her be for awhile, she likes being with people, even if she's sound asleep. Sometimes, I'll be holding her while lying in our bed, and she'll fall fast asleep in my arms. Rather than put her in her crib I let her sleep in between Albert and me. She's such a precious angel. No trouble, either. She sleeps through the night, no fussing — unlike one of you. Not mentioning any names, daughter Ruth."

James continued with his concerns.

"It's been well over two months, it seems hard to think that a baby could be born in this world and not be noticed or missed."

Albert was strong in his reply.

"But son, she was noticed and would be sorely missed by your mother and me if she was suddenly gone."

"Daddy, that's not what I mean and you know it. Yet I have to admit that it seems like she was supposed to be found by you. And boy, is she thriving."

James reached over and gently moved Grace's head to what he thought to be a more comfortable position.

"She took over your heart, Daddy, for sure, and yours too, Mama."

Henna responded to her son-in-law.

"Is that such a terrible thing, to have your heart taken over, James? Besides which we had to put our hearts in the space to be taken. Isn't that so Albert?"

"I know it's so and so does he, " Albert said,

As he tapped James' side with a broad sweep of his massive arm.

"Do you think for a moment that each and every one of you didn't take over our hearts when we first laid eyes on you? And isn't that what love is all about? What good is it if you don't give all of your heart to those who bring you joy?

"Why, I can't help but smile anytime I think about a member of this family. The warmth that you all give my soul makes me hungry to wake up in the morning, and gives me peace and comfort to fall asleep each night.

To know that God has given me so much love from all of you makes me want to give it to the world, and my world, outside of this family, grew, the day I found Grace. There's something special about her. Henna knows what I mean. Grace has brought us a renewed sense of our love. Even with all the grandchildren around and still coming."

Albert smiled broadly at Betty.

"This house is filled on a round-the-clock basis once again, with the joy and love that only a new life can bring. I honestly hope that no one ever comes forth and claims Grace. My heart would be sore for a long time if that was to happen."

Henna gently lifted the sleeping child out of the swing and held her close. She whispered her words, so as not to wake Grace, nor to give her words any weight.

"No one is going to claim this child. No one is going to take her from us, Albert. And who, in their right mind, would take this child away after they can obviously see what good care we have given her. Do you think that they would just hand her over to someone who just left her to die on the side of the road? I don't think so, Albert."

Henna turned and walked into the bedroom to put Grace in for her nap. She approached the crib and with her free hand turned back the blanket.

She gently put the sleeping Grace down on her stomach and covered her. Henna let her hand rest on Grace's back, stroking her ever so softly. Tears filled her eyes, and began to roll down her face.

"I won't let anyone take you from us, baby. You deserve all the love that Albert and I give and we deserve you. God gave us a wonderful, beautiful gift when you came into our lives. When He tells us to let you go, then we will, but not until His words speak loud and clear in my ears. Do you hear me child? Loud and clear."

But the thought that this child might one day be taken from them kept flashing into Henna mind as she rejoined her family and finished the rest of the day. Not until she and Albert were in bed that night, did she let herself cry aloud. Albert held his wife of 38 years in his arms, not quite sure what to say or do to comfort her.

He stroked her back as he held her body tightly against his own. His own fears were building and he fought hard to hold back the swell in his throat.

"Darlin', we have to believe that Grace was meant to come into our lives, for us to care for and love. Why would I have found her the way I did? Why didn't we just turn her in the very first day?

"That's what the Henna and Albert I know would have done — the correct and sensible thing. What we did, we did from a knowing deep inside each of us and I believe it came from a power that is guiding us each moment of the way. I'm not going to stop believing in that power now, Henna, and please, darlin', you must continue to believe in it, too."

"I have faith, Albert. I know the same things that you do, but I have this feeling that one day we're going to have to give Grace up. Not because we want to, but because we are suppose to. Because that is the plan that God has for our Grace."

Albert took in a long deep sigh.

"If that's to be, then when the time comes we'll both know it. Just like we both knew we were to keep her rather than turn her over, but I don't think that's gonna happen for a long time Henna. I don't think we should lose worry over such a thought. Close your eyes, darlin', let me sing you to sleep, just put your mind and heart to rest for tonight, Henna. Morning will be here before we know it."

Albert continued to hold his wife tenderly in his arms, stroking her back and singing in a low hypnotic tone. He sang "Amazing Grace" with such tenderness that the notes hung only moments in the air.

As his arms filled with Henna, he had no choice but to let his tears flow quietly, but steadily down his face. Henna listened to Albert and could not help herself from easing the thought of losing Grace from her mind, but easing her heart was another matter.

Without knowing, I carried you.
Without knowing,
I surrendered you to the earth.

RACHEL

*T*he smell from the kitchen was so awful that Rachel had little choice but to breathe it in. She tried to cover her face with her pillow but it did not help.

She knew what was coming next. She anticipated the fight between her mother and her mother's current boyfriend.

She braced herself for the screaming and cursing but before she buried her head, she lifted her pillow quickly to see if her little sister was still sleeping.

She was. Six-year-old Stephi's little form was curled up in a tight ball at the end of the bed they shared.

She wondered how Stephi could sleep so soundly. When Rachel was Stephi's age, she'd been unable to sleep through all the fighting that went on.

She remembered when the police came and broke up the fights between her father and mother. One time, when she was about five, it had gotten so bad that both parents had landed in jail and she in the foster care system.

Foster homes weren't too bad at first; oh, she missed her mom and dad, but she didn't miss the fighting or all the other stuff.

She stayed at the first home for a couple of weeks then when they needed a place for a baby Rachel had to go elsewhere. That's when she went to Mama Goldman's house. Foster care at its best.

Rachel let out a sarcastic laugh. Mama Goldman was a witch, to say the least. And her son Marvin? Well Marvin, was something else. He made her do things to him that made her sick to her stomach. He'd force her to suck his ugly thing, just about as often as he could corner her in any spot in the house.

At first she would scream, cry, and fight him. When he belted her hard enough to blacken both of her eyes, she figured it was useless so she gave in without a struggle. No one was going to help her so she might as well stay quiet and let him do what he wanted. He could not really touch her. Not really — not in her special place, the spot that only she knew about.

Her Mom didn't even know about this place. It was a place, like one of the beautiful islands in that place called Hawaii.

Only Rachel knew about this secret place. She found it along time ago. She found it when her Mom locked in her closet for three days without food or a place to pee.

It was always pretty and always safe in her special place and she could go there whenever she needed to. She went there when things got too loud or too painful.

So, that's where she traveled to, whenever good old Marvin trapped her in a corner, in that wretched place called Mama Goldman's house.

She went there a lot in the six months it took her own mother to get out of jail and another six before they were reunited.

She was sure things would be better when she and her Mom moved into their new apartment that the state welfare worker had found for them; and they were, for a little while anyway.

It didn't take more than a few months before her Mom was back on drugs and screaming and hitting her again. Her Dad never did come back; that's when the boyfriends started; boyfriends that stayed over night most of the time.

Rachel had to admit that although it was hard at times, at least it was home, and at least it was her real Mom.

Then, the following year, things got quiet for a while. Rachel didn't have any idea what was happening except that she did notice that her Mom was getting fatter. Then after awhile there was this sweet, little baby girl, who they named Stephanie. Her Mom even stopped using drugs, or at least that's what Rachel thought.

Then Stephi began to fuss. She would start wailing at the top of her lungs and nothing her Mom did could quiet her. Her mom started getting mad at her crying all the time. One day Rachel saw her mother slap her sister hard across the face because she wouldn't stop crying. She raced over to her baby sister and picked her up.

"I'll take care of her, Mommy. You go lay down."

Rachel held her little sister, rocking her back and forth in her arms, like she saw on TV and the baby stopped crying. From that day, forward Stephi became Rachel's responsibility, her baby.

She didn't mind at all, in fact she loved feeding and bathing her, she took care of her as though she were her own. Her Mom hardly did anything for either of them anymore. She took to going out at night and not coming back till early morning, leaving them alone. As scared as she thought she should be, Rachel somehow felt safer with her mother out of the apartment.

She would change and feed Stephi and the two would settle in for the night snuggling close in the same bed that they shared at this moment six years later. At 14, Rachel was more her mother than her sister.

Rachel's thoughts were interrupted when she heard her mother's voice begin to swell in volume. She could hear the drugs taking over her speech as she slurred her words.

"Get the fucckkk outa mmy house, youuu fuckkking ppprick."

Rachel pulled the pillow tightly over her ears and began to hum. The fight escalated. She sat up and switched her position in bed so that she was now snuggled close to Stephi. She covered her protectively with her arm and pulled the sheet over both of them. She grabbed her pillow with her free arm and again tried to smother the noise coming from the kitchen.

Rachel quickly thought of a plan of action in case things got out of hand. If the fight moved into their bedroom, she would need to have a safe place for her and Stephi.

Out of the line of fire, so to speak, she would tell her little sister jokingly and she wasn't so much concerned for herself, it was more for Stephi.

After all, she was still a baby, and as far a Rachel's thinking went, she was her baby. The responsibility was overwhelming at times, but she took it on all the same. Someone had to, otherwise she knew all to well what would happen to her sister.

The state would come in and take her away. They would put in her a place like Mama Goldman's; in a place that someone like the likes of Marvin might be. Rachel would rather die before she let that happen to her Stephi.

As those words flashed in her mind, a picture filled her thoughts of another baby, but this one was tiny and whimpering, she in a dark place somewhere.

Rachel tried to think about it harder. She pressed her eyelids tightly together to squeeze out a clearer picture. She tried to capture the setting of where she saw this baby.

A set of bright lights, headlights maybe, she thought, took up space in her mind's eye. Rachel gasped. She sat up quickly.

The word, "No," escaped her mouth. She covered it with her hand and lay back down next to Stephi.

Rachel's eyes were wide open now. She looked up at the ceiling and tried to think clearly.

What had happened four months ago? There was bleeding that wouldn't stop; it had scared her.

She had had her period for a year, but this was different. And she had been so sore, as though someone had ripped her up the middle. She figured that one of her mother's boyfriends had done something to her when she was sleeping, but she could not remember or figure out how that could have happened since she was always so careful to protect herself and Stephi. But something had happened to her, something she couldn't remember.

She hadn't told anyone about it, especially her mother, because it didn't matter. It was not as if anyone was going to do anything about it. Rachel just took care of herself and remained quiet.

The bleeding had stopped after about 10 days and the soreness left her body as well. Rachel had felt an ache in her heart though, and that she couldn't seem to get rid of no matter how much she played with or took care of Stephi.

However, now she understood. Now for the very first time, she realized what had happened to her. She had had a baby, in the lot near Bresco, behind the waste container. She put her hand, which was now a small fist, into her mouth. She tried to stifle the cries from her throat; her mind raced.

She remembered how angry she had been when the car lights had flashed by, allowing her to see what she had pushed out of her body.

It was a baby. She had not even known she was pregnant. She'd figured her period stopped because she hadn't been feeling so good and she was throwing up all the time. Her belly had swelled up all the sudden and she thought she had a tumor or something.

She'd been afraid to tell anyone. She'd feared they would tell her she was going to die. That was when the true fear set in, when she thought of what would happen if she'd no longer been there to protect Stephi from world in which they lived. So she hadn't told anyone and when the pain started, she knew she had to handle it alone.

It started around six o'clock in the evening. It was kind of an ache in her back. She couldn't get comfortable no matter what position she was in.

By one in the morning, she was in agony. The two of them were alone as usual, and Stephi was in a deep sound sleep. Rachel paced back and forth in the living room of the tiny apartment, not knowing what to do.

Another hour passed, and she felt like she was going to die if she didn't get some air. Rachel peeked at Stephi and kissed her gently on her head.

She was about to do something that she had never done before; she was going to leave her little sister alone in the apartment. She knew their mother would not be back till the next day, at the earliest, so she her laid her hand on her little sister's back, took a deep breath then left the room.

Rachel paced around the small living room and into the kitchen but nothing helped. Her belly kept getting real hard and then soft again. Every time it hardened, searing pain shot across her whole mid-section. The pains came closer together and each one felt worse than the one before. Rachel thought walking down the stairs of the building would help it go away; maybe some air.

They lived in the P.T. Barnum Apartments on Bird Street. It was not the safest a place to be in the daylight, let along walk to alone in the night — something Rachel had never attempted.

She quietly opened the door of the apartment, locked it behind her and headed down the stairwell. She reached the outside of the building and moved as quickly as she could down the sidewalk, grabbing her hardening belly as she tried to walk.

She had no idea where she was walking to but kept moving south.

She could smell the foul odor from the waste plant. She was going to head toward the small park across the street and near the Convent, but a barking dog quickly followed by an angry man's voice, made her change her direction. She turned and headed south toward the Bresco lot. She lifted the broken fencing that surrounded the plant and made her way through, then lowered her self down behind one of the container.

Her body was now in spasm every few minutes and she lifted her long tee shirt and pushed down her shorts to place her hands on her bare belly. Rachel rubbed her belly and cried. This was more pain then she knew what to do with and she did not know how to get rid of it.

She felt an uncontrollable urge to push. She squatted down and pushed as hard as she could causing a pain that ripped up between her legs. She was on fire with the pain.

A car was coming. She tried to lie flat; she covered her belly with her arm, trying to hide herself.

The car passed by without stopping. Rachel lay on her back, pulled her legs up and held on tightly. The urge to push came over her again as another searing pain shot across her middle and the burning, tearing feeling between her legs intensified.

Rachel pushed and pushed until she felt something bulging out of her. Her belly softened and she reached down and felt between he legs. There was something protruding out of her, a mound of mushy wetness.

Her belly hardened again and Rachel bore down; suddenly she felt and heard a plop between her legs. She sat up and reached between her legs and then her belly hardened again; she pushed again and something else fell out of her.

Another car came toward her this time the headlights provided enough illumination for Rachel to see what she had pushed out of her body. She glanced down as the light swept quickly past the spot where she half sat, half lay.

She gasped. She covered her mouth with her hand, and bit her lip to hold in her scream.

"Noooo, this is not real...a baby, a baby lying between my legs!"

Rachel turned onto her side and got on her knees. She began to rock back and forth, moaning in her agony. She began to retch. The sweat ran off her body, mixing with her tears. She screamed in pain.

"A baby, I can't take care of another baby. I can't do it!"

Rachel slowly stopped rocking and got angry. She stood up, full of rage and lifted her small fists to the sky.

"I won't do it; I won't take care of it."

She let out an angry sob, "I can't, I can't, I can't."

She lowered her arms and turned away from the oncoming set of headlights. She walked angrily, with her fists clenched at her side, back to her apartment.

She did not turn around once, or wonder for a second what would happen to the baby that she had just given birth to in the Bresco lot. She moved as quickly as she could to the one who depended on her every moment of the day.

Now, nearly four months later Rachel was remembering what had happened that night. She lay there next to her little Stephi, listening to the sounds diminishing from the kitchen. She heard the door slam and the apartment filled with silence.

"Good," she whispered aloud as she removed herself from Stephi's grasp.

Her little sister had wrapped her own arms around Rachel's middle and had thrown one of her legs over her protector's.

Rachel sat up and slipped off the end of the bed. Walking into the small living room, she looked around to see if her mother had passed out somewhere or had left the apartment, as she hoped.

Rachel was alone in the living room and the kitchen was empty. She extinguished the still-burning cigarette one of them had left in the ashtray on the counter.

She opened the refrigerator and surveyed the contents. She would need to go to the store later, for milk. Rachel opened the cabinet to the left of the refrigerator and reached behind the few cans of vegetables on the second shelf.

She had taken to hiding food stamps in different places throughout the apartment; places where she could keep them safe from her mother who sold them for drugs. She counted the coupons.

Good. They would be okay, enough till next week, when the next month's supply was available.

Rachel looked around the tiny kitchen and felt sick at the mess her mother and boyfriend had made of the place. She had worked so hard yesterday cleaning the place up. Knowing that the social worker was supposed to come today, she began again to make the apartment presentable.

At the same time, she began to replay the pictures that had only moments before filled her head. She thought about the baby; not the one, sleeping in the other room, whom she had taken care of for the last six years, but the one she had just come to realize that she had had by the side of the road four months ago.

Was it alive? Was it a girl? A boy? What if her child had died? Did that mean she would go to jail?

Just recently in the news there had been a story about a girl the same age as she who had given birth to a baby girl.

Too afraid to tell, the girl had tried to hide it from her family and so she had set it outside on windowsill, the baby girl had fallen three stories to her death.

Rachel couldn't remember if they arrested girl for killing her baby or not. She did recall something about how the mother had contributed to the death of the child, but she wasn't quite sure what that meant.

If Rachel's baby had died because she'd left it on the side of the road, did that mean that she had caused its death?

Rachel began to panic. She sat down on the sofa and drew her skinny legs up to her chest. She pulled her tee shirt over them, then wrapped her arms around herself. She lowered her head, resting it on her knees and began to cry.

How had it come to all this? How had she gotten pregnant in the first place? She stayed far away from boys and they didn't give her a second look. She was very thin and under-developed, certainly nothing to look at for the boys in the neighborhood.

The only time she'd had any breasts at all was toward the end of what she knew now was her pregnancy. Afterwards, her breasts hurt something awful, and although she told no one, they leaked.

Out of her nipples came this thin white liquid; of course, it went away after a couple weeks, but for awhile she was sure, something was seriously wrong.

Now, she was again skinny and flat chested, not the kind of girl to attract a boy's attention.

She also knew how to stay clear of her mother's boyfriends. She made sure they did not touch her and especially watched if one played too close attention to Stephi.

Only once had one of these men gotten too close. It had been one night when Rachel had not been able to sleep, so she'd gotten up and tiptoed into the kitchen for a drink.

Mom had passed out on the floor of the living room, and her boyfriend appeared to be asleep on the couch. When Rachel returned to the bedroom, she froze in her tracks; there standing over the bed, where Stephi was still sleeping, was this creep. He was rubbing himself and looking at her little sister.

Rachel returned to the kitchen, reached in a drawer for the longest knife they had and returned in a flash to the bedroom. She stood in the doorway and with clenched teeth, hissed, "Get away from her."

The man turned quickly and saw this skinny little girl wielding a knife at him. She looked pathetic and even though he knew with one rap across the head he could probably knock her out, if not kill her, he raised his hands.

"Okay kid, don't worry, I'm leaving. I didn't touch her — honest."

He walked slowly toward Rachel, who backed up to let him pass and held the knife in a threatening position until the man walked past her and out the door of the apartment.

From that moment on, Rachel kept the knife under the bed, just in case, she thought.

Just in case.

She never used it again, but the thought that the knife was there made her feel less afraid.

Rachel had learned early about sex. She had caught her mother a couple of times with men, so she knew how babies got made.

What she couldn't figure out was how her baby had been made. Was it even possible to make a baby without a man? Had she somehow picked something up in the public restroom of the nearby park?

Then even worse thoughts crossed her mind. *What if someone had done something to her when she was asleep?* Or maybe he did it but she was so afraid that she blocked it out of her mind, just as she'd done with her own baby?

Rachel lifted her head and brushed away the tears from her face. This was not going to help. She tried to think rationally but the only thought was that the baby had died and that she would be held responsible. She stopped thinking for a minute to listen for the sounds of Stephi waking up.

The clock on the wall read 7:30. Stephi walked into the room and greeted her with a big yawn.

"What are you doing up already?" Rachel was hoping to be alone for a little while longer, to figure out what to do about the baby thing.

"I missed you. I turned over and you weren't there, I got scared, RaeRae."

"Come here, silly. I didn't go anywhere. Do you think I would go somewhere and not take you?"

Rachel quickly flashed back to four months earlier, to the one and only time she had left Stephi alone.

"No, you wouldn't do that, but I still got scared, RaeRae. Where's Mommy? Is she gone already? Or didn't she come home yet?"

Even at six, Stephi knew her mother well. Rachel tried to make light of it.

"She went out real early this morning, before I even got up. She made a mess in the kitchen, which we had better clean up before the lady from welfare comes. We can't have her hinking we live like pigs."

Stephi had already curled up next to Rachel and rested her still-sleepy head on her shoulder.

"Do we have to? Can't we let Mommy clean it up? She made the mess, we should leave it for her."

Stephi spoke with a defiant tone. She showed her anger at their mother much more easily and readily than Rachel did.

"You know, RaeRae, sometimes I wish Mommy didn't live here. Sometimes I wish it were just you and me."

Rachel knew that her sister spoke words that she never had the courage to say out loud.

"But she does live here, with us, and she's not going anywhere. Maybe she'll get better; maybe someday she'll be able to take care of us. For now, kiddo, we've got to take what we have."

With that, Rachel began to tickle her sister, who tried to defend herself. They ended up giggling, falling into a heap on the floor.

"Okay, to work!" Rachel stood up and pulled Stephi hands to land her in a standing position as well. Together they made their tiny apartment as presentable as possible.

Later, when the doorbell buzzed, Rachel – knowing exactly who was calling — glanced around, quickly surveying the apartment before opening the door.

She looked Stephi over quickly and last, but not least herself. She had to create the image that they were being well cared for, as was the apartment. She was not going to risk going back into foster care for anything.

They would separate the two of them for sure and there was no telling what would happen to Stephi. No, she had to make certain that everything was just right.

Thank God her mother was not around. Rachel knew she would not show up during the interview. In fact, they probably wouldn't see her till the next day.

She took a deep breath and opened the door. Ms. Harley stood there with a smile on her face and a briefcase in her hand. She extended her right hand.

"Hello, Rachel, how have you been? And Stephi how are you, sweetie pie?"

She patted Stephi's head as she walked through the doorway and into the living room. She continued her journey through the four-room apartment trying to be casual about the mandatory check on the living conditions of welfare recipients. She felt that at times, it was such an invasion of their privacy; but in this case, she really did care how these children were living.

She had seen so many people try and beat the system. Sadly, children like Rachel and Stephi often got shortchanged.

They should have been living in a better apartment, but this was all the monthly allotment would afford them.

As she looked into the cabinets and into the refrigerator, Mrs. Hanley let her thoughts wander about the girl's mother.

Where is she this time? I wonder what excuse Rachel will have for her absence today. "Things look nice and clean, Rachel, you've been working hard. Where is your Mom this afternoon? I really was hoping I would get a chance to speak with her."

"She's out working on a church project. They're collecting canned foods for the shelter and Mom is volunteering to carry cans." Rachel did not miss one word of her much rehearsed excuse. Nor did she flinch when Ms. Harley began coughing upon hearing it.

"That's nice, dear. Thank goodness for people like your Mom. She's always involved in some good work." She looked at the younger child. "How is school, Stephi? Is everything going okay? You both get the breakfast and lunch programs right, Rachel? It's so important for children to eat properly so that they can do their best in school."

"Yes, Ms. Harley, we get the breakfast and lunches. They're good aren't they, Stephi?" Stephi nodded obeying Rachel's strict instructions not to speak until she gave her the okay sign. Otherwise Rachel was to do all the talking for the both of them.

"Stephi is doing fine in school. Of course we've only been back a short time, but he likes her teacher a lot, don't you Stephi? I like mine, too."

"Stephi, would you mind if I talked with Rachel alone for a few minutes? Perhaps you could go in the kitchen and draw a picture that I can take back to my office. I would love a picture to put on the wall near my desk."

The younger child looked at her sister and when Rachel gave an almost indiscernible nod, she smiled and stood up and went into the kitchen.

"Is there something wrong Ms. Harley? Is there a problem with our...getting...food stamps and the other help you give us? I mean if there is I'm sure my Mom could straighten things out. You can tell me what I should tell her to do and she can go down to the state building tomorrow."

"No, Rachel, there is no problem with your benefits, but I'm afraid there is a problem. Rachel, exactly where is your mother? Tell me the truth. Is she using drugs again, honey, is that it?"

Rachel hung her head down then picked it up quickly. Tears were in her eyes. She looked directly at Ms. Harley.

"My Mom is not back on drugs. I told you where she is - she's at church. Please Ms. Harley you have to believe me." Rachel was almost pleading. Ms. Harley took her hand and patted it.

"Rachel I'm only trying to help. I have a feeling it's you who keeps this place looking so nice, and Stephi in clean clothes. I think you do the shopping and just about everything else around this place. I know you are only trying to protect your mother, but you're only 14 years old. My God, Rachel you're a child raising another child. It's not fair, to you, to Stephi or believe it or not to your Mom. If she needs help, protecting her will only delay that. If she's not able to take care of you two girls, I need to step in and do something about it."

The two of them sat there, neither knowing what to say at this point. Ms. Harley broke the silence.

"I have to give you credit, you are doing a remarkable job. I don't know many 13...14-year old girls who could take care of a six-year-old, a home, and go to school at the same time. From what your teachers tell me you're very bright to boot. It's just not fair. Rachel your whole childhood is being taken away from you. Doesn't it matter to you? Aren't you angry about it? I know I would be if it were me."

Rachel sat on the couch. She kept her head down, so that Ms. Harley could not see her tears. As she listened to her speak, she wondered if maybe she could ask Ms. Harley about the baby. Rachel pushed the thought from her mind. Not now, maybe she would call her at work tomorrow. She wouldn't give her name; maybe she'd just ask some questions — like, how does someone find out if a baby left on the side of the road is alive or dead? Would anybody even know?

"Rachel? Rachel, dear, are you okay?"

Ms. Harley lifted the child's chin and looked into her eyes. She could see that they were brimming with tears. How badly she wanted to make things right for her, but, honestly she was at a loss as to what to do.

If she fully reported her findings, the girls would be in foster care immediately and more than likely, The Department of Children and Family Services would separate them. She did not know who that would be harder on Rachel or Stephi.

She stood up to leave. She held onto Rachel's hand as she walked the short distance to the door. "You have my number? You will call if you run into any problems, if things with your Mom get out of hand."

She turned before she left and embraced the skinny young girl who was trying so hard to be brave and strong. She left saying softly under her breath. "It's not fair, it's just not fair."

Stephi entered the room. "Is she gone? Are we safe? Did I do okay, RaeRae? Did I do like you told me to?"

"You did just fine, Stephi, just fine, and yes we are safe, at least for awhile. We just have to keep are noses clean and stay out of Mom's way, so she won't get mad and start hitting again. But if that happens, and I don't think it will so don't you worry 'cause I'm here right? We'll be okay. Really, I promise. Haven't I always taken care to make things okay for us?"

The smaller child wrapped her arms around her sister's middle. "Yes, yes, yes. I love you, RaeRae. I love you to pieces."

~ ~ ~ ~ ~ ~ ~ ~ ~ ~

The wind howled, sounding throughout the desert as if it were calling the old woman by name. Returning from the cave at twilight, Gyada let the sound of the wind carry her home. She was tired. She had begun making nearly daily visits to the cave since the child had been born. She would sit in the belly of the cave all day, keeping a vigil on her thoughts.

The wind felt warm against her old and worn skin. She held her head up to allow her namesake to feed her spirit as she moved steadily closer to her hut. Suddenly she stopped. Looking up to the north of where she stood, searching the sky for a sign. They were calling to her.

The northern sky filled with a burst of brightness that illuminated the desert beneath it. The wind swirled around Gyada with more force, almost lifting her upward. She stood with both of her feet planted in the cooling night sand of the desert. Tears filled her eyes as she felt the words coming from the light in the sky into her heart.

"But she is a child herself; what will she do with the memory? Where will she go?"

The woman, lifting her head to the bright northern sky, raised her eyes and ears. She turned her head listening carefully for answers, hoping for direction in her mission.

When the sky grew dark again and the wind died down, she lowered her head and journeyed back to her hut. She stood in front of her firestones and stirred the ashes with her walking stick. From her standing position, she blew into the middle of the cold ashes.

Within seconds, a red glow appeared in the middle of the stones. The wind gently picked up Gyada's breath urging the red embers brighter and stronger.

Gyada leaned forward slightly, with both hands she held onto the carved, worn head of her thick walking stick. She rested her head on her right arm and stared into the fire that was rapidly growing before her. Her only thoughts were of the words she had heard in the cave.

Her heart grew heavy; such pain for one so young and still more to come.

The apartment was still, absent of noise other than the sound of Stephi's steady breathing. Rachel sat in the dark in the living room wondering what the next day would bring.

Had they convinced Ms. Harley last week that their mother was taking good care of them? Rachel could only hope that when the social worker came the next time her mother would be in better shape and able to talk to the social worker herself.

Rachel's thoughts drifted to the baby. She wondered what had happened to it. Maybe it is still there. Maybe there is a trace of it, or a body. What if someone found it and it's still alive and okay?

Rachel felt hopeful for a moment or two, but then the reality of what she had done hit her. Again, she spoke aloud to herself, but in a much deeper darker whisper.

"It can't be alive. I let that poor baby die, alone."

She let out a sob and lowered her head, covering her face with her small hands.

"God, I am sorry. I didn't mean it, honest." Her bony shoulders heaved again and again with each muffled sob. Suddenly, the door-knob rattled. Rachel could hear her mother's voice outside of the door of the apartment.

"Goddamn son-of-a-bitch. Where's the fuckin' key. She's got the fuckin' door locked again."

Rachel wiped her tears away quickly and ran to the front door. She unbolted the door and opened it to see her mother half-standing, half-leaning against the wall of the hallway.

She was not alone. With her was a man that looked as stoned as her mother was. Both reeked of alcohol. Her mother's clothing was half on, half off, her blouse partially buttoned, and her jeans unzipped.

"Shhh, Mom, be quiet, Stephi's sleeping. Let me help you."

Rachel reached for her mother, placing an arm around her waist and the other taking her hand. Before she walked her mother through the door, she turned to the man.

"Please, you can't come in; my sister's really sick and I think it's contagious. She has been throwing up and having the runs all day. In fact I'm still cleaning off the floor."

The man covered his mouth and made a retching sound.

"Catch ya later, babe, I can't stand no shit and puke."

He turned and stumbled down the hallway to the stairway.

Rachel helped her mother to the couch, and then quickly returned to the door. Closing it quietly, she slid the dead bolt in place, just in case her mother's friend changed his mind and came back. She turned and looked at her mother who was slouched on the couch in a stupor, appearing more dead than alive.

"Mom, let me help you get to bed."

Without waiting for a response, Rachel went about removing her mother's clothing. She held each piece she touched between her two fingers and tossed it into one heap. Mixed with feelings of love, anger, and disgust, she got her mother to lie down on the couch and then covered her with a blanket.

Rachel gathered up the dirty smelling clothing after throwing a towel around the pile.

"Why can't she get better? Why does she do these things to herself?"

Rachel thought to herself, as she placed the pile of clothes in the pillowcase that had long since become the laundry bag for her mother's clothing; she kept Stephi and hers separated just in case.

After checking the door one more time, and making sure her Mom was covered, Rachel returned to her own bed and tried to get some sleep. She lay there with her eyes opened, looking up at the peeling ceiling. The feeling that something was about to happen kept pushing its way into the pit of her stomach. Rachel could not put a finger on it, but she felt a rush of fear every time she thought about her mother. She closed her eyes and prayed aloud.

Please God, help me. Help me make things okay around here. I'm afraid. I'm scared. Something bad is gonna happen. I know it. I need your help, please."

As the tears rolled down her cheeks, Rachel turned on her side and put her arm around her little sister. She pulled her close and slowly drifted off to sleep.

~ ~ ~ ~ ~ ~ ~ ~ ~ ~

"How's Betty feeling today? She looked mighty big on Sunday. Maybe the Doctor is wrong with her due date. I think she's about ready to have that child." Albert was full of questions and his own opinions regarding his daughter-in-law's condition. Henna listened and laughed at some of her husband's remarks, others called for her stronger tone.

"She'll have that baby when the good Lord wants her to and not a minute sooner. You need to stop making comments every time you lay eyes on her; there's nothing worse than a man telling a woman about things he knows nothing about. For goodness sake, Albert, don't you have enough to do with Grace in our lives now?

"I'm only offering my opinion, woman. There's nothing wrong with that and after all, it is my grandbaby she's carrying around. And you're right, we do have a lot to do with Grace here but not so much that I can't be concerned with a new life that's about to enter into our family."

Changing her tactics, Henna put her arms around Albert's waist and looked into his eyes.

"Why don't you take yourself down to the plant and see if they need you for anything? I know you had a lot of time off accrued but land sakes Albert you hardly work anymore. I gave my notice at work, so I could take care of Grace, but there's no reason that we both have to be here all the time. Don't you miss the boys?"

She knew her man only meant well. He was only talking out of concern for Betty and her unborn child, but good Lord he tried her patience's at times.

"Maybe you can take Grace for a walk. She'll be up from her nap any minute Al, she'd love it."

Henna held tight onto Albert's middle, swaying ever so slowly.

"I know when you're trying to get rid of me Henna; I can see through your sweet talk like a piece of thin ice. You know I don't mean to make a pest of myself I'm just worried about Betty and the baby. She don't look right, Henna. I know I don't have to tell you that. I know you've been worrying about her too."

Albert clasped his hands around Henna back. He began to sway with her. They stood there for a moment holding each other close. Henna rested her head on Albert's chest and began to hum softly. She could feel Albert's heart beating strong and steady. She could feel his warm breath against the side of her face as he embraced her more tightly. She began to feel the passion in her body begin to rise.

With their bodies pressed so close together, she could tell that Albert was beginning to feel his own passion stirring. She lifted her head and leaned back, Albert's strong arms supported her.

Looking into her husband's eyes she spoke quietly, "Maybe Grace will sleep for awhile longer, if you can keep your moaning low enough, my sweet man."

Albert leaned down and pressed his opened mouth onto Henna's awaiting lips. He moved his hands up Henna's back and slowly under her arms and to her breasts. Holding them for a moment, he could feel them swell in his hands.

His hands traveled up her neck, resting his strong hands on either side of her face. As his tongue explored her mouth, Henna let out a soft moan. Slowly, he began to move them both forward, toward the bedroom and just as Albert was about to unfasten the last button on Henna's blouse, a playful baby giggle was heard.

"Sweet Jesus, that child is just like Susie was as baby. I swear they know when I'm even thinkin' of a little lovin'."

Henna laughed softly, "It does seem like they have an unusual timing, don't it, darlin'. Well, you just wait till the sun sets tonight and that child is tucked in nice and tight. Whoa, baby, you better look out."

Now Albert was laughing, tucking in his shirt and roaring in hysterics.

"You gotta date, sweetheart, and mind you, I'm gonna take that child outside in the fresh air all afternoon. She's gonna be sleeping like a log, before seven."

As Albert was finishing this last sentence, Henna had already returned to the room with Grace. She was wide eyed and all smiles and holding tightly to her little brown bear, the one that Susie had tucked away in the bags of clothing she had brought over a couple months back.

"Well don't you look happy and where do you think you're going, missy? You interrupted a big moment. Did you know that?"

Albert stretched out his arms and lifted Grace away from Henna.

"Don't think I'm not going to remember that, either. You just wait, when you're not looking."

Albert lifted Grace into the air and kissed her rounded tummy. He blew raspberries over and over until Grace was giggling out loud.

Henna stood back and watched the two. She could not help but laugh along with them. She folded her arms across her chest and held onto herself, as though she were trying to hold onto the moment itself. Her eyes misted until she blinked them clear. She hoped that Albert hadn't seen her slight shift in spirit.

Henna still could not completely clear away the feeling that Grace was not theirs forever. No matter how sweet the moment, and there were so many of them, she was still fearful at times of losing Grace. She didn't know how Albert would handle that; she didn't want to think about what he might do.

She loved Grace from the bottom of her heart, but Albert looked at her in a way that Henna had never experienced before. He looked at her differently than he had his own natural born children or any of the grandkids for that matter.

"Henna, you here, darlin'? You look 500 miles away. I know what you're thinking. Look Henna, this child is staying right here and nobody is going to take her away from us. Right, Grace?"

Albert pulled Grace close to him and kissed her cheek.

"Don't mind me, I'm just chasing cobwebs out of my brain. You get Grace dressed and I'll get her stroller ready. I'll make her a bottle to take along just in case."

She reached over and gently squeezed a soft round baby cheek.

It had been just over five months since Grace had come into their lives. Henna thought she and Albert had a full life before, but now it was not only fuller but richer as well.

As she filled up the baby bottle and warmed it just so under hot water, her thoughts once again traveled toward that of Grace's biological mother. She wondered where she was. She wondered if she even thought about the tiny baby that Albert had found nearly dead by the highway.

Albert and Grace interrupted her thoughts.

"Okay, we're ready. I took along an extra blanket just in case it got any cooler. This winter has been kinda mild but you never know when a strong cold wind is gonna blow. We'll be home before supper. I think I'll head toward the park. Maybe we'll stop by and visit Albert Jr. — how's that sound, sweetie?"

He gave Grace's cheek a tap after tying the bow of her knit hat, under her chubby chin.

"If you stop, remind him about his job for the shower on Sunday for Betty. He's supposed to take her out for a while so we can set up and surprise her. Don't mention it if Betty's there. Albert, we've all tried to keep this a secret — unless you've already spilled the beans. Goodness knows, you've never been the one to hold onto a secret."

"Now that's unkind and unfair, Henna. I've only slipped two or maybe three times, and none of them has been completely my fault. I swear, people see me coming and — "

"Hush, Albert. Go on, get a move on, or it will be dark before you leave. I know and you know that you've got a, a, I won't say big mouth, that wouldn't be kind. It sure is good size; large enough to let things slip right out."

With that, she pushed Albert out the back door, playfully slapping his bottom. He turned and smiled broadly at her. Henna watched as the two of them made their way down the driveway. She called out after them,

"And don't say nothing to Betty about her size, her weight, her due date, nothing."

Albert turned as he reached the end of the driveway. "Can I at least say, 'Hello,' or would you rather I not open my mouth at all?"

He half-waved, half-brushed her remarks away. "See you later, darlin'."

~ ~ ~ ~ ~ ~ ~ ~ ~ ~

Al Jr. scolded his very pregnant wife.

"I thought the doctor told you to stay off your feet the rest of this week? Betty, you've only got another few weeks, please baby, listen to the woman, she told you, you need to take it easy or you could go into labor early."

He reached for the filled laundry basket.

"I'll do this, go lay down on the couch and put your feet up."

He led his wife to the sofa and gently but firmly pushed her down into a prone position then lifted her swollen feet onto a pillow at the other end. He looked at her as he sat down on the floor next to her. This pregnancy was truly a gift from God; however, it had taken a toll causing his nightly prayers to be fervent for his wife and child's safeguard.

"I am tired. I wish things were as easy as they had been with Elizabeth. I know I was nine years younger, but I thought I was in pretty good shape before I got pregnant. I don't remember feeling this weary towards the end."

She rubbed her swollen belly with one hand and patted Al's cheek with the other, and as if she were reading, his mind said.

"But we'll both be fine, I know it. You're right I just have to be more careful and truly follow the Doctor's advice. There's a lot depending on my taking care of things, isn't there Al?"

He nodded, unable to think what he and Elizabeth would do should anything happen to her.

"You bet there is and I am going to see that you do just that. You're staying put until dinner and then I'm going to carry you upstairs to the bedroom. Elizabeth and I will go rent a movie and we can all get comfy in our room and watch it. I'd say we watch it alone but Elizabeth's feeling something's going on and I know that she'd be sad and lonely if we left her out."

"She'd be sad and lonely? I can't wait to get back to being a full time mom to her. I miss our shopping trips. We have such fun together. Even when we don't see eye-to-eye, which is getting more frequently these days, I still love my baby. By the way where is she?"

"She's riding her bike out front."

I told her not to go too far, just in case, you know. I mean you never know just when you're going to burst, right?" They both began to laugh, continuing even as Elizabeth came running through the front door, followed by her grandfather and baby Grace.

"Look who came over to visit. Grandpa's walking to the park. Can I go with him, please? "

"Child, you sound like a whining horse. Of course you may go, just behave yourself and mind Grandpa understand?"

Albert leaned over and kissed Betty's cheek.

"How are you doing? Anything yet? Whoops, I'm sorry; I'm not supposed to ask you that. In fact, I've got strict orders not to mention anything about the baby or anything at all for that matter. But ears that aren't here can't hear, so what's cooking? Why are you lying down? Oh my God, are you having pains? Is this it?"

Al, took hold of his father's arm.

"Daddy give us a break, we still have a little ways to go yet. And believe me you'll be one of the first to know when Betty goes into labor."

He stood up, pulling himself up with the help of his father's strong grip. "The Doctor just told her to stay off her feet, that's all. Everything is status quo Dad. But it won't be long, right honey?"

Betty smiled up at her husband.

"No, it won't be long — in fact I think I could go anytime now. Not that I'm in labor or anything, but I'm sure as hell ready otherwise. We are all anxious to have a new baby in this house, and just as sweet as little Grace. Right, guys?"

Her husband and child agreed loudly and in unison.

Grace smiled and waved her arms from her vantage point on Albert's shoulder when she heard her name.

"Okay, let's hit the park, while we still have sunlight to shine on us."

Albert turned to Elizabeth. "Get your coat, sweetie. Son, give me a hand a minute with the stroller, its front wheel is stuck or something."

As the two men walked outdoors, leaving Betty alone on the sofa, Elizabeth ran and gave her mother a kiss.

"Bye, Mommy, now stay put, and let Daddy wait on you hand and foot. I love you."

Betty returned the kiss and hug and laughed at the seriousness of her little girl's tone.

Meanwhile, on the front walk, Albert pushed his son for more information about Betty's condition.

"Are you telling me everything, son? Your Mama is worried sick over Betty. Is there anything we can do for you? How about if we have Elizabeth come and stay with us? That would make things a little easier, wouldn't it?

"Or maybe you could all move in with us. Mama is home all the time with Grace. This way, she could take care of Betty, should anything happen while you're at work."

"Whoa, Daddy, thank you for caring, but really we're okay. Honest. And Betty will be fine if she just stays off her feet for the next few weeks. As far as Elizabeth staying with you, I think, she'd be mighty upset if she weren't around to put her two cents regarding her Mama's care. But, thanks Dad, I know you're only speaking out of love."

"Okay, son, but know the offers stand anytime you need to call on them. Oh, by the way, Mama wants to know if things are still set for the shower on Sunday. If Betty has to stay off her feet maybe, we should cancel it."

"Oh, I don't think we have to cancel it, but maybe we might have to change things a little. I'll call Mama later, while Betty's napping, we'll figure something out. I think Betty would love the baby shower. We'll just work around this little set back."

He turned to walk up the steps of the front porch. "Have fun with the kids! See you in a while."

Elizabeth, who had already taken Grace and put her in the stroller, was halfway down the sidewalk by the time her grandfather joined them on their journey to the park.

Al entered the front door and called to Betty.

"Honey, you want a cup of tea or something else from the kitchen?"

There was no response from the living room.

"Sweetie, how about a cup of tea?"

He was not prepared for what he saw. Betty was stretched out rigid on the couch. Panting rapidly, she was bent back in a strange position, her head jerking awkwardly to one side and her arms flailing spastically. He was at her side in a second, watching in horror as his wife convulsed in front of his eyes.

Then all movement ceased. As rigid and spasmodic as she'd been seconds before, Betty was now as limp as a rag doll.

Her breathing remained rapid. Drool spilled down her chin. Al took her wrist and found her pulse running wild. Placing a hand over her chest, he could feel her heart pounding much faster than he knew it should be.

Something had just gone terribly wrong. He had to get help and he knew that Betty would die right in front of him if he did not get her to the hospital fast.

He grabbed the phone and dialed 911, and rapidly explained the situation to the dispatcher, pleading with them to hurry. Then dialing a number requiring no thought, he held his breath waiting for Mama to pick up.

With a shaky voice he spoke into the phone. "Mama, it's Betty, I need you. I called 911, they're sending help."

He started to explain.

"Son, listen to me, get a hold of yourself; go back to Betty, I'm on my way."

Seconds later Henna grabbed her purse, car keys and coat and was backing out of the driveway, praying as she quickly drove the short distance to her son's house.

Henna could hear the siren of the ambulance as she sat holding the still limp hand of her daughter-in-law.

With a cold washcloth, she wiped the sweat from Betty's brow. Al Jr. was kneeling on the floor next to his wife, who seemed to be fading further and further away from him.

He told Henna how he had found her, and not knowing what else to do or say, he just knelt there and silently cried, stroking his wife's arm.

He put his hand on her belly and he felt a weak kick from their yet unborn baby.

"Mama, the baby's still alive — it just moved. Oh, God, Mama, I can't lose her! I can't think about life without her... Elizabeth... Mama, what will she do...? Oh, Jesus! "

He sobbed into his wife's hand that he grasped with both of his own.

Henna put a hand on her son's head.

"Don't waste those tears on the living. Use that energy for some prayers. She's still with us and so is the baby, you just said so yourself. Listen, I know that it is going to be okay. I don't know why. But in my heart, I know that God is with us."

At that moment, the ambulance pulled up in front of the house.

Al raced to the door and guided the rescue crew in. They began to work on Betty, asking him questions as they went along as the EMT crew lifted her onto the stretcher, one of the crew looked at him, "You want to follow us or ride in the back?"

Al was in a daze, Henna answered for him.

"Albert Jr. you ride with Betty. I'll stay here and wait for your father. Then I'll come right over to the hospital once I get things situated with the children. I'll call Susie and Ruth; they can help with the kids."

Henna was standing by her son, with her arm around his waist as she spoke. As the stretcher with Betty on it rolled past them and out the door, she turned and took her eldest child in her arms.

"Now you listen to me, she's going to be okay, you've got to believe that, you've got to call on the strength and faith that God gave you."

She took her son's face in her hands and as she brushed away the tears that were streaming down his face, she kissed him, holding him tightly.

Henna wished with all her heart that she could take the fear and pain from her son but knew that all she could humanly do was share in it. She watched as Al climbed into the back of the ambulance and the attendant slam the door shut.

Wiping the tears from her face, she returned inside to make the calls and wait for Albert and the girls.

~~~~~~~~~~

"Sonofabitch"

Unsure of how much time had passed Rachel startled awake at the sound of her mother's voice as the woman stumbled around in the kitchen. Cabinet doors opened then slammed shut. A dish crashed to the floor followed by a glass.

She thought about to getting up to see if she could calm her but hoped her mom would find what she was looking for and then leave for the day.

Suddenly she heard a very angry, "What the fuck?" but before she had the chance to move, her mother was in their room waving the food stamps in her face.

"What the hell are these? Why have you been hidin' stamps from me? Get up. Get the fuck out of bed, you sneaking little bitch."

Rachel's mother grabbed a handful of hair and pulled her daughter out of bed. She dragged Rachel over Stephi, who was now wide awake and full of fear.

"Mom, please, I only put them away, not to hide them from you! Honest! Please, Mommy, let go, you're hurting me. I was going to tell you where they were. Mommy please... stop!"

A raised hand slapped Rachel soundly across the face, sending her to the floor.

"You lying bitch. You weren't going tell me about these. You were keeping them from me. I'll teach you to keep things from me."

She pulled her foot back then savagely kicked Rachel in the middle of her back.

"Mommy, don't hurt RaeRae!" Stephi screamed at the top of her lungs as she jumped on her mother's back and began to strike at her with small angry fists.

"Leave my sister alone! I hate you, I hate you I wish you would die and leave us alone!"

The woman turned and picked up her youngest child and threw her across the room. Stephi landed in a heap after slamming sickeningly into the radiator. The little girl lifted her head, then dropped it banging it soundly on the floor.

"Oh my God! Mommy... what did you do? Stephi, Stephi..."

Rachel looked up at her mother with intense rage. In spite of her own pain, she crawled to her little sister and tried to see how badly she was hurt. A great deal of blood was beginning to pool around her head.

Rachel's mother stood there, frozen in place.

"I didn't mean to hurt her. Rachel, please, I love you! I love Stephi! I didn't mean to hurt her. Ya gotta tell them that. Oh my God, what am I gonna do now?"

She sat on the bed, holding onto her head, swaying back and forth, she continued to cry and talk to herself.

"Stephi? Stephi? Answer me… Are you okay? Can you hear me? It's me, RaeRae."

Rachel was choking back her tears, as she pleaded with her little sister to respond. She brushed Stephi's hair out of her eyes. Blood was trickling out of Stephi's mouth and ears.

"Please don't die, Stephi! I love you. Please don't leave me! "

She turned her head and looked at her mother, screaming at her, *"You've got to help me, help Stephi, call 911. Do something, anything. Stop crying and help me, Mommy please! Do something for Stephi. "*

But Rachel's mother continued to rock back and forth, mumbling and crying about how hard she tried to be a good mother, complaining that nobody helped her, that she had to take care of everything and it was too much for her to do alone.

Rachel stood up and ran to the phone in the kitchen. She dialed the three numbers for help and screamed into the phone for assistance. She gave the address of their apartment and told them what little she could about Stephi's condition, then pleaded for them to hurry before she hung up the phone and returned to her little sister. The pool of blood around her head was now at her shoulders.

Rachel had brought back a dishtowel and tried to wipe the blood from Stephi face. The more she wiped the worse her sister's face looked, blood was smeared all over her now. Rachel spit on her hand and began to wipe her little sister's face, like she did when she need a quick clean up.

"Stephi, I love you, look what a mess you're in. Mommy will make you clean. Let me wipe your face. Stay still, baby."

Stephi's blood covered Rachel's hand without thinking she brought the hand to her own face to wipe away the tears that freely spilled, now her own countenance took on a grotesque, bloody appearance.

Rachel heard loud sounds coming from the hallway. There was someone banging on the door. She raced to open it allowing the EMT's and police in all at once. They followed her back into the tiny bedroom, where Stephi lay in bloody heap and their mother had collapsed on the bed.

Rachel knelt by her sister, covering her with her thin arms.

"Please help her, I tried to stop the bleeding, but I can't. I can't wake her up, either. Please, make her wake up."

An EMT gently took Rachel's hands and lifted her to a standing position.

"You have to let us near her. We can't help her unless we can look at her and see where the blood is coming from. I promise we will help her, but you have to let us near her, okay? Why don't you go tell the Officer what happened. Who did this to your sister? He has questions to ask you. Isn't that right, Officer?"

The EMT turned to the policeman next to him, who shook his head yes. He extended his hand to Rachel who took it weakly. He led her out of the bedroom. Rachel turned and said in a quiet voice.

"She doesn't like needles."

Rachel followed the police officer into the kitchen. He sat her down at the table and looked around the kitchen for a cloth or towel. When he found something, he went to the sink and soaked it with warm water. He returned and knelt before Rachel and began to wipe the blood from her face.

The questions began.

"What's your name, honey?"

"Rachel" Her voice was barely audible.

"That's a pretty name. Well Rachel, can you tell me what happened? How did your sister get hurt? What's her name, sweetie? I think I heard you call her Stephi. Is that it, Stephanie?"

Rachel nodded, tears rolling down her face.

"How old his she?" The officer kept asking questions, which were answered with only weak responses from Rachel.

"Can you tell me what happened honey?"

Softly and quickly, Rachel shared the last 15 minutes of little sister's life.

He called to another officer. Rachel heard them whispering, not caring much about what was being said regarding her mother. She only wanted to know how Stephi was. She watched in silence as her mother was handcuffed and escorted out of the apartment between two policemen. She opened her mouth to ask about Stephi when she saw the EMT pull a sheet over her little sister's still bloodied face.

"*NOOOO, SHE CAN'T BREATHE IF YOU DO THAT!*" She ran to the stretcher and pulled the sheet out of the attendant's hand. She laid her face next to Stephi.

"It will be okay Stephi, Rae Rae's here. I won't let them scare you. I know you don't like your face covered. You want me to sing you a song, Stephi?"

As she held onto tightly to her little sister's lifeless body, Rachel began to sing, "Rock a Bye, Baby."

She stopped singing, and looked at her sister's face.

"I love you, Stephi."

She wiped her sister's face with her hands. She took the corner of the sheet and wiped away as much blood as she could from Stephi's face.

"There, that's better. Now you look better. I've got to show them how good I take care of you. I do take good care of you, Stephi, don't I? Rachel laid her head back down on her sister's chest and began to sob.

"*I'm sorry, Stephi. I couldn't stop her. I'm sorry...I'm so sorry...please...don't leave me, please...*"

The EMT gently put his hands on Rachel's shoulders, pulling her off Stephi's body.

"We've got to take her, sweetie. You've got to let us. She's gone. There's nothing you or anyone else can do."

He put his strong arms around Rachel, holding her gently but firmly. The three others in the group wheeled the stretcher through the small apartment and out the door, closing it behind them.

Rachel stood completely still, watching them, until the sound of the door closing startled her.

"*NOOOOO, I HAVE TO GO WITH HER!*" She began to sob and scream. The screaming stopped suddenly and her voice became a whisper.

"She'll be all alone! She won't like that. She'll be — I'll be all alone."

The attendant who was still holding her put his face next to Rachel's cheek.

"I'm sorry, honey, I gotta go with the ambulance. I'll be with her. I promise I'll stay with her as long as I can — as long as they let me. But I have got to go, now."

The man hugged Rachel, and left her alone with two policemen.

"Where going to take you to the hospital to make sure you're okay. Did she hurt you?"

It was hard to tell if all the blood on Rachel belonged to Stephi.

"I'm okay. She only hit me a little. She threw Stephi across the room, she hit her head on the radiator. That's when she started bleeding. I tried to stop it, but I couldn't."

Fresh tears started to pour from Rachel's eyes.

"You did the best you could sweetie — didn't she, Mike?" The other police officer nodded in agreement.

"You sure did. But I think we should take you to the hospital and have you checked out, just to be on the safe side. Okay? And is there anyone we can call? Do you have any relatives? Where's your dad? Grandparents? Anyone who we can call to meet us there and maybe you can stay with till things get sorted out?"

Rachel nodded her head no. There was no one. Suddenly her fear was huge. The horrid face of Marvin, from Mama Goldman's, flashed in her mind.

"I won't go back there! Please, you can't make me go back there. Please, don't take me back there."

The look of panic on her face sent chills up the spine of both men.

Rachel stood up, suddenly remembering Ms. Harley. She ran to the cabinet and found the card Ms. Harley gave her on her last visit. Maybe she would take her. She seemed to care about her. At least that was the feeling Rachel had gotten, when she gave her the card.

"Can you call her? She's the social worker from the state building. She's been keeping track of us for a while. She told me I could call her if I ever needed help, if things ever got too much for me to handle."

There was a pleading tone to her voice. One of the policemen took the card from Rachel and walked to the phone. He called the number, spoke quietly for a few minutes, and then turning to Rachel he relayed the message.

"Ms. Harley said she would meet us at the hospital. She wants you to get checked out. She said she'd be there in 15 minutes. Okay?"

Rachel nodded in agreement. Not knowing if she'd ever be back in the apartment she asked if she could bring some things with her.

"That's a real good idea, honey, but only a few things, okay? We don't have much time. You need any help? "

"No, I'll only take what I really need."

With that, she returned to her bedroom. She kept her eyes purposely away from the spot where Stephi had landed. She opened her dresser and threw a few things on the bed in a heap. She opened the drawer of the small table she and Stephi used as a nightstand. Inside was a picture of Stephi, taken last year by a friend in the apartment building. She gave it to Rachel when she saw the smile on the child's face.

Rachel looked at the picture now. Her eyes filled up again, but she quickly stopped herself from feeling all the pain in her heart. She put the picture on the top of the pile of clothes that she planned to bring along with her.

She took the pillowcase off the pillow on the bed, the one that Stephi had slept on. She lifted it to her face and could smell the scent of her little sister. She picked up the picture and set it aside and stuffed the rest of the things in the pillowcase. She picked up the picture and held it tightly in her hand.

"I'm ready."

She opened the door and walked out of the apartment; she did not look back.

~~~~~~~~~~

By the time they had arrived at the hospital, Betty had seized another time. Albert watched in horror as his wife convulsed on the stretcher. She was still convulsing as they entered the ER.

Their obstetrician was waiting for them at the door and quickly stabilized Betty's condition with various medications. After explaining the situation to a very worried husband, she told Al she needed permission to deliver the baby by Caesarean section.

He signed the consent form in a daze, praying he was doing the best thing for Betty as well as the baby.

Within 15 minutes, a nurse came back out and told him it was over and he now had a beautiful son.

He asked how Betty was doing and she assured him that she was in good hands and that they were trying to stabilize her. Henna and Albert arrived at the hospital only minutes later and he shared with them the news.

All sorts of feelings were in Al's heart as he talked to his folks. Betty was not out of the woods and he knew very little about the condition of the baby, only that it was a boy, and it was alive.

Henna and Albert comforted their son, waiting and praying for good news to be on the lips of whoever told them what was going on behind those closed doors. Shortly thereafter a nurse came with words that made them all smile, if not only for a moment. The baby boy was in excellent health and they could see him; Al, Jr. could hold his newborn child.

Now, six hours later, their son was in an incubator and Betty was stable. Her vital signs were normal and steady. They placed her in ICU to keep a close eye on her, and now she was beginning to show signs of coming out of it.

For several hours he sat by her side, praying she would open her eyes. Praying that his wife would come out of what the Doctor had described as post seizure unresponsive state, a result of pre-eclampture, the cause of her convulsions.

Al leaned his head on the railing of her bed, holding tightly to her hand; he could not stop his tears from flowing. Suddenly, Betty emitted a soft moan, and she squeezed Al's hand.

"Betty? I'm right here honey. I'm right here. You're going to be just fine and the baby is okay; more than okay, he's perfect. Open your eyes, sweetheart, please, look at me. We have a son."

Al leaned close to Betty's ear when he saw that she was beginning to stir.

She fluttered her eyelids then opened them slowly, scanning the room trying to figure out where she was. Al continued to speak reassuringly. "Honey, you're okay. You had the baby. It's a boy, Betty. And he's beautiful." Al was desperately trying to get through to her.

Betty's eyes had a frightened look. With all the wires attached to her, it was hard to find a spot to touch. Betty opened her eyes and smiled at her weeping husband.

"A boy? We have our son? Where is he? Is he okay? What happened?"

Al wiped his tears, kissed his wife repeatedly, telling her the incredible events of the past six hours.

"Shhh...Sweetheart, it's okay. You went into some kind of seizure and they had to perform a cesarean section to deliver the baby quickly. Betty, we have son. And he's just fine. And so are you, thank God. "

As Al was reassuring Betty, her doctor approached the cubicle. "Excuse me for a minute Al, while I check Betty." Al stepped outside the cubicle space as the nurse with the Doctor quickly pulled the curtain around the bed. Within seconds, her hand pulled the curtain opened.

"Well, let me tell you how well you are doing considering the scare you put everyone through, woman. I'm going to transfer you to the OB floor so you can be near your beautiful new son. Who, by the way, I hear is coming along just fine. I'll sign the orders and check in with you tomorrow."

She turned to leave, and then looked back at Betty and Al.

"I hope this is it for you two. I know I can't take any more delivers like this one but congratulations on a job well done!"

"You can bet your life on that, Doctor. This is it; unless you want to bury me six feet under, after I drop dead from fright."

Al reached out his hand and spoke as the Doctor took his hand into her own. "Thank you, thank you for giving me back my wife and saving my child."

The next day Betty's hospital room filled with both flowers and visitors. Al made five different trips to the nursery window trips with family and friends.

Unable to grasp how small and perfect his son looked, he lost count of how many times he went to look at the boy on his own..

The baby was now in an isolette like all the other babies in the nursery and making frequent trips to their mothers for feeding.

The first time the baby came to Betty's room, the joy was palpable. Elizabeth, bursting with excitement and anticipation could not contain herself.

"Can I hold him first? Please?"

Betty put a finger to her lips to quiet her then spoke gently to her husband who she knew had endured much during the last hours.

"Al?"

Al leaned over the isolette and picked up his son. Cradling him in his arms, tears began to fall from the grown man's eyes. The little baby was lost in his father's arms. Al walked over to Betty's bed and sat next to his wife.

Elizabeth joined them on the other side, kneeling so she could see all that was going on.

The three of them sat there looking in amazement at the tiny baby boy who was beginning to take up a great deal of space in each of their hearts.

Betty opened her arms to receive her new son and Al gently released him.

She carefully undid the blanket that swaddled him warmly and little arms and feet suddenly appeared. Elizabeth gently touched a tiny foot.

"Oh, Mama, he's so little. Look how tiny his feet are. He's so cute."

She kept oohing and aahing, while she stroked her little brother's foot.

Al traced his finger down his son's arm to his tiny hand. He placed his pinkie in his son's hand and it quickly closed around it.

"He's holding my hand, Betty, look. What a grip. He's strong. That's my guy. You show 'em how tough you are. We're going to be tossing a football soon."

"Oh goodness, Al, let the poor child at least learn to crawl before you make him a quarterback. He does look strong though, doesn't he?"

"Mom, can I hold him? I'll be careful."

Betty smiled and picked up her son and placed him in Elizabeth's arms.

"He's so little, Mommy. Was I this little when I was born? Was I as cute as.... Oh my goodness, what are we going to name him? He's got to have a name. We can't keep calling him the baby. How about Jeffrey? That's the name we talked about, Jeffrey Adam. How's that sound Daddy?"

Al smiled first at Betty and then at the sight of seeing his two children.

"What do you say, Betty? Do we stick with Jeffrey? It's got a nice sound, good and strong. Jeff. I like it. Hey Jeff, toss me that ball. Yeah, I like how that sounds."

"Well, I guess it's settled."

Betty took hold of Al's hand and put her other on her child. "Jeffrey Adam, welcome to the world."

~~~~~~~~~~

"I can't wait to get out of this gosh darn suit. I feel like I'm wrapped up tighter than a rubber band. Why'd I have to wear a suit? It's not Jeffrey's gonna mind if I went to his baptism in my comfortable pants and sweater. Do you really think he'll notice if I have a tie on or not, woman?"

"Listen, old man, you're wearing that suit and tie to the church even if the Lord Almighty Himself comes down from heaven and says you don't have to. You're not gonna die or suffocate as you put it, just cause you have a nice suit on your body. You look wonderful Albert, what in God's name is wrong with you? You'd think I was asking you to slice off your right hand or something; you go on and on enough to make a woman crazy.

Albert stood up straight and pulled on the lapels of his suit jacket.

"I do look nice, don't I? I guess it won't kill me for a couple of hours. But I'm telling you, I'm bringing along a pair of nice comfy sweats to change into at Al and Betty's. A man can suffer just so long Henna. Isn't that so, baby?"

He bent down and picked up Grace who sitting on the floor of their bedroom. Now 11 months old, , she crawled around pretty much where she wanted. She was pulling herself up and hanging on to things, trying every so often to take a step or two. Now she was waving her arms, giggling at Henna and Albert. She knew already, that their voices were not angry.

"What has Mama made you wear? I bet you wish you didn't have to wear that fancy-schmancy dress. Well we'll just have to make her happy, now won't we, darlin'? I suppose we could do that for someone as special as your Mama, right?"

"You had better stop talking nonsense to that child Albert. Everybody knows little girls just love to dress up. Isn't that right, precious?"

Henna patted Grace's bottom and planted a kiss on her cheek.

"Okay, you two, let's get a move on. Albert, is Grace's bag all set? Do you think we should bring the portable crib? What if she falls asleep? Did you put in the extra jar of food like I told you to?"

"Henna, for gosh sake we're only going 10 minutes to the church and then 10 minutes away to Al's house. If Grace falls asleep, I'm sure

Betty won't mind her sharing Jeffrey's crib. After all, they are only babies. You want me to bring our pillows and blankets, just in case?"

Albert began to fill the bedroom with his hearty laughter.

"Oh sure, poke fun at me. Remember, it's you who is going to make a trip back to the house if we need something, understood? Men!"

The three of them headed out the door, with Albert carrying everything but the kitchen sink; or so he thought.

The church service took no more than 20 minutes and then the whole family returned to Al and Betty's for a celebration.

On the drive back, Grace fell sound asleep in her car seat, giving Henna space to chastise Albert properly.

"See, I told you we should have brought the crib along. What if Jeffrey is asleep too? Then what are we going to do smarty pants?"

"Oh, for goodness sake Henna, so the two kids sleep in the same crib for an hour or so. It's not like Grace is going to hurt him or anything. The most she could do is roll over him and by the looks of Jeffrey; he probably wouldn't even feel it. What's he weigh now, 18 pounds? We're not talking a lightweight child here, Henna. Relax, you worry too much woman."

As Henna and Betty placed each sleeping child on either end of the crib, they smiled at the peaceful sight. Betty closed the blinds and tiptoed out behind Henna to join the family downstairs. Henna entered the living room and announced to the crowd, but looked at Albert as she spoke.

"The two babies are sleeping, let's keep the noise down or whoever wakes them up is minding the two of them the rest of the day. Do I make myself clear?"

"Henna, when have you not been able to make yourself *loud* and clear?" Albert's emphasis on the word, "loud" had the group in stitches.

"Daddy, I'd watch my step if I were you. Mama's nostrils are flaring — a sign of danger if I recall my childhood."

Al Jr. patted his father on the back and as if not to offend, his mother ran over and gave her a loud kiss on the cheek.

"Don't you try and butter me up, Albert, Jr. You are as bad as your father – worse at times! Now sit and behave like gentlemen."

Al hugged Henna one more time.

"Oh, Mama, I'm teasing. You know that I love you." He then turned to the men and boys in the room. "Okay, you guys, how about a game of touch football? This way we'll be out of Mama's hair and the house."

The room filled with laughter once again, which slowly faded as it emptied of men and children; the women headed into the kitchen.

"Betty, Susie, and I are thinking of joining that new health club. They're offering two-for-one, maybe if you join you can help us convince Mama to come along."

Ruthie talked as she poured coffee for each of the women seated around the kitchen table.

"I'm not joining a health club. I'm in as good as shape as I care to be for my age, thank you very much. I am not putting on spandex pants and a tiny tee shirt for no one. Your father thinks my body is just fine. Can you just hear his mouth if I was to join a health club and wear those type outfits? My Lord the man would have a heart attack."

The three other women were holding their sides with laughter. The idea of Henna in spandex and the reaction of Albert was too much for them. Even Henna, couldn't stop her self from giggling.

The sound of the laughter traveled upstairs and filtered into the room where the babies were asleep. Grace's eyes fluttered. She stirred into wakefulness. Lifting her head, she looked around to see where she was. She turned herself over to see the familiar little horses that hung over her in Jeffery's crib.

She wriggled her toes under the covers then kicked her legs around and freed herself from the blanket that Henna had so carefully place over her.

Now what could she do? She sat up and was surprised to see Jeffrey at the other end of the crib.

Quietly she crawled to the other end to investigate. Grace sat next him, hoping he would wake up so she could play with him.

She leaned over him, listening to him breath. She could feel his warm breathe on her face.

She smiled. Grace loved Jeffrey. He made her feel inside like Albert and Henna did when they held her. She filled up with joy. Grace crawled back to the other end of the crib. She held onto the railings and pulled herself up to a standing position. She let go and stood there. She ventured a foot forward. It worked. She was still standing. Okay, now the other. Her left foot followed the right and still she stood.

Hesitantly she moved forward, with her arms stretched out for balance, she made her way to the end of the crib where Jeffrey was still asleep.

Now she really had to wake him up. She had to show him what she could do. Grace bent over and put her face close to Jeffrey. Something was different. There wasn't any warm breath coming from him. The baby under the blanket was still. Grace put her hand on Jeffrey's face and rubbed him gently but he didn't move like he usually did when she touched him. She rolled him over.

Grace moved her tiny hand to Jeffrey's heart. She held it there and closed her eyes. Suddenly a warm brilliant light emanated from the child and her small hand now placed on Jeffrey became very warm. She felt a flutter and then a stirring. Jeffrey took in a long deep breath and then expelled it.

Grace opened her eyes but continued to lay her hands on the baby. She watched as he opened his eyes and began to move his arms around; he smiled up at her and she smiled back. Grace tenderly took hold of Jeffery's hand and lay down next to him, then both babies drifted back to sleep.

I will find you.
I will come for you.
Listen for me in the dark of night.

RACHEL

*P*lease, Ms Harley, isn't there someone else that will take me? Somewhere else I can go? It's been three months I can't stand it here any longer. I try, really I try, but I can't seem to do anything right. The other kids here do things to each other. Please, Ms. Harley."

Eleanor Harley listened to the words of the teenager whom she had known for nearly three years.

Her heart ached for Rachel, but her hands were tied. This was the third foster home she had placed Rachel in since her mother was sent to prison for killing her little sister. Rachel tried to no avail to fit in somewhere. Ms. Harley knew she had to learn to adapt.

"Rachel, you know I don't have any other place to put you, right now. Honey, you have to give the people a chance. They really are nice, you know. I wouldn't send you to a place that wasn't nice. Maybe, some of the other kids behave in ways they shouldn't, but Rachel, they've had a hard time of it just like you, honey."

Trying to change the topic, she asked, "How's school?"

"Okay, I guess. It's almost out for the year. I'll be in high school in September. Ms. Harley, have you heard anything from my Mom? Has she written me any letters?"

The arrangement made by protective services stated that any correspondence from her mother had to go through Ms. Harley.

"No, honey, nothing yet. Maybe once she finishes the drug program in prison and is able to deal with what she did, she'll be able to write to you. I can't promise you anything, Rachel."

Ms. Harley couldn't for the life of her understand why any of these children, who had endured unspeakable acts of cruelty by parents, would still long to have them in their life.

"Did you send her my letter? Does she know that I forgive her? I wish I could go and see her. Do you think I could, I mean would they let me?"

"Of course they would let you, but Rachel, your Mom is not ready to see you yet. You may have forgiven her, but she has to forgive herself and that's going to take time, honey. Be patient, please. Listen, sweetie, I have to run, I have a meeting in five minutes. Is there anything I can get for you? Anything you want or need?"

"Just to leave this place, that's all. I don't need or want anything else."

Rachel's voice was soft and sad.

"I'll come by next week to see you. Be patient and remember I'm thinking about you."

Rachel hung up the receiver and stayed put at the kitchen table. Her foster brother Willie came into the room without Rachel hearing. He came up behind her and put his hands on her face. He covered both her nose and her mouth, making it impossible for her to breathe.

He put his mouth close to her ear and whispered in a menacing voice, "You've got such a big mouth, why don't you use it for something worthwhile, bitch."

Rachel tried desperately to pull his hands away but he was much stronger than her. She panicked. She needed air. Her eyes widened in fright and she struggled to free her self. Suddenly Willie's hands were gone. She sucked in air as she tried to wipe the smell of him away from her face. She heard her foster mother's voice in the hallway.

"Who left the door open again? I told you kids this is not a barn. Close the damn door. I can't stand the damn bugs that fly in here. The next person who doesn't shut the door will be sleeping in the back yard. I need help out here so anyone within ear shot, better get their tails down and give me a hand with the groceries or no eats tonight."

Within seconds, Rachel heard five sets of feet clambering down the stairs. She stood up, went to the kitchen sink, leaned over and splashed cold water on her face. As she was drying herself with a paper towel, her foster mother walked in the kitchen with two bags of groceries.

"Didn't you hear me ask for help?" Rachel turned around quickly, "I'm sorry, I was on the phone with Mrs. Harley. I didn't hear you Mrs. Bentley."

"Well, if you want to eat tonight you had best get yourself out to the car and help the others with the groceries. And didn't I tell you that you're not to call that woman when I'm not here. I don't want you telling any stories about me. I won't stand for any of you kids telling things that are not true."

"I didn't say anything about you, honest. I just wanted to know if she had heard from my Mom, that's all." Rachel started to walk out of the kitchen past her foster mother to end the conversation. Her foster mother was not the one to listen to Rachel's heartaches. She was not in the least bit interested in her pain.

Rachel passed the others in the hallway and said nothing to them. She ran to the car and got a large bag filled to the brim with food and struggled to lift it. As she pulled it toward her and turned around, she felt a breeze sweep past her.

It was gentle, and warm with a sweet scent. The breeze lifted Rachel's bangs off her forehead. She stood there waiting for something to happen. She glanced upwards; there in the early evening sky was a circle of light.

It glistened in brightness, shooting a ray downward encompassing Rachel where she stood. The light swallowed up Rachel and as quickly as it came, it left. A voice filled her from within and she listed intently. A smile rose in her heart and moved to her lips. She lowered her eyes and a tear ran down her face. Rachel looked up toward the sky and knew that her heart would soon find peace.

Supper was long over and it was bedtime for the six children who lived at the Bentley foster home. Rachel was in the bathroom washing her face when the door opened and a younger girl named Sabrina ran in.

"I gotta go, I gotta go." The words rushed out of the child's mouth and Rachel mind was filled with the face of Stephi. Tears filled her eyes and she quickly splashed more water on her face.

"That's okay, Sabrina, you can come in."

The small child relieved herself, then wiped and flushed as Rachel finished at the sink. She patted her face dry and left the towel neatly on the rack. She helped Sabrina wash and dry her hands before scurrying away to her bed. Rachel turned the light out in the bathroom and closed the door behind them.

The room they slept in was at the end of the hall and was shared by the two other girls currently living in the home. There was no chatter, not the typical young-girl conversation of boys and make-up and school heard in the cramped room. Each girl climbed into her respective bed to end yet another day in foster care. A dark-haired girl whose bed was nearest the light closed the day.

A full moon spilled light into the room through the window causing the branches of an old oak tree to cast shadows on the wall next to Rachel's bed. She took her finger and traced the outline of the branch. She climbed the tree several times and knew the feel of the bark.

She felt it now. She felt her legs lowering herself downward. Maneuvering through the branches, in her mind she quickly reached the ground. Rachel left her hand on the wall and closed her eyes. A smile crossed her face and she closed her eyes and fell into a light sleep. Soon. It would be soon.

Several nights' later Rachel lay in bed with eyes wide open, her breathing was light but steady.

She listened. The house was still. The television was no longer on downstairs. There was no noise coming from her foster mother's room. She held her breath for a moment then quietly slipped out of her bed. The moon provided more than enough light for her to gather her belongings in her pillowcase.

The picture of Stephi was snuggled in the middle of the few pieces of clothing she owned. Rachel pulled on a pair of jeans and a shirt then put on her sneakers and walked over to the window. She made rabbit ears then tied the pillow case closed and stuffed it under her shirt then tucked her shirt into her pants.

She quietly pushed the window up to allow her passage and the oak tree greeted her with open arms. She reached for the closest branch. The bark was rough, but welcoming, and then quickly made her decent.

Rachel touched the ground and stood there for a moment, looking upward to the sky for direction. She passed by the tree and walked down the driveway to the road.

As she walked, she took the pillowcase out from under her shirt and swung it over her shoulder. She headed into the night feeling better than she had in a long time. She wasn't exactly sure where she was heading but knew she was heading to place she had been before. She let her heart guide her every step as she walked peacefully into the night.

Rachel walked the long journey back through her old neighborhood and headed toward Bresco. The moon continued as her guide. She sniffed there was hint of garbage. The closer she got the stronger the smell. A wave of anxiety washed over her.

What if? She pushed the unfinished thought away. She quickened her pace as she neared her destination. The smell had not improved since she had visited this place over a year ago. The reflection of the streetlights that bounced off the fencing helped her locate the opening.

She went in, heard a scurrying noise and stopped in her tracks. Rats. Thoughts of the baby washed away and calmness beset her. She looked around and saw nothing. She retraced her steps to back outside of the fence, then leaned back and waited.

~~~~~~~~~~

The sky was now a dark purple; the day was close to beginning. Albert's car was nearing the entrance to 95 as he headed to work.

Now that Grace was in their life; he left for work nearly an hour later each morning. He'd perform his morning ritual, then begin each day holding and rocking and talking to the child, softly singing hymns to her.

The early morning stillness helped him to glance over the past year of his life. Grace had filled he and Henna with such joy, he could not imagine life without her. God had entrusted to him a most precious gift and he knew that he would do anything to honor such a reward.

He glanced suddenly to the right, the headlights of his car lit on something leaning against the fence that surrounded Bresco. It only took a moment realize it was a young girl, and another to know that he must stop. He pulled his car over to the side and shut off the motor.

His mind raced back to the morning he had found Grace. A familiar feeling washed over him. He looked at the girl then closed his eyes for a moment. A smile crossed his lips and he nodded. He opened his eyes knowing exactly what to do.

As he opened his car door, the girl began to walk toward him. He could see her face and knew instantly who she was. He walked to greet her and then stopped, letting her walk to him in her own way. Somehow he knew he had to make her feel safe.

Rachel walked slowly toward the man. She listened as the voice inside told her that he was the one. That this man knew where her child was and that he would help her. She reached Albert and looked into his eyes. Before she could speak, Albert extended his large hand to her and spoke quietly.

"My name is Albert."

Her hand was swallowed up by that of this big gentle man. She felt a tenderness in his touch that she had never felt before.

"I'm Rachel," she said softly. "Are you the one...the one who found...?"? Tears rolled down her face and onto her shirt, she could not continue.

"Yes darlin', yes, I'm the one who found your child Rachel. You had a little girl. Her name is Grace."

Rachel let out a small gasp. "Alive? A girl and she's alive?"

"Oh, honey child, that is one tough little baby girl you gave birth to. I found her right where you left her.. I took her home to Henna. Henna's my wife."

"Where did they put her when they took her from you?" Rachel was fearful of the answer thinking of her own experiences with foster care.

"Nobody put her anywhere. She's still with Henna and me. Still smack dab in the middle of our hearts."

Albert's smile was wide and full of pride.

Rachel lowered her head to hide the tears she could not hold back. But unlike the last time, these were tears of joy. She held onto Albert's hand, afraid to let go — afraid the moment was only a dream and she would wake up.

Albert sensed her emotion and reached to wipe her tears away. He softly brushed his large hand across her cheek and heard a muffled sob escape from the girl's throat.

He gently put his arms around her and pulled her close to hold her. Her shoulders heaved with heavy sobs as she let out some of the pain of the past year. He let her cry until she quieted herself. She pulled her head away and looked up at him.

"Is she really alive? I was so afraid she had died. That I had left her alone to die. I didn't want her to die. I just couldn't take care of her."

She lowered her head again onto Albert's chest. He continued to offer her comforting words.

"You did what you had to do child and God took care of the rest." What's important is that she is alive and well and that you are here right this moment. Would you like to see her?"

Albert asked the question without any hesitation, knowing it was the only thing to do.

"You mean you'd let me see her? I wouldn't cause any problem, I promise. I mean if you want I'll just look from a distance."

Rachel could not imagine seeing her baby. What would she look like now? The only picture she had in her mind was that of a tiny, whimpering mound that had fallen out of her last year. What did she look like now? She was more than a year old.

"Of course you can see her. I know Henna and she would not let me rest one minute if I came home and told her I found you and let you get away. Why she'd make me search every house in the city for you. You'll like Henna, Rachel. And does she love Grace. Grace. How perfect the name for she was given to us by the Grace of God."

Rachel moved away from Albert and wiped the back of her hand across her face.

"I won't cause any problems; I just want to make sure she's okay. Do you live far from here?"

"No, just a few miles back. Come on let's go so you can meet her, our little Miss Grace."

The ride took only a short while but long enough for Rachel to relay her story to Albert. She choked back tears when she got to the part of Stephi's death but swallowed hard and pushed on.

She told her tale quickly, not looking for sympathy just throwing out the words as though not connected to their meaning.

Albert could feel her ache and he drove a little faster, knowing he had to get this child to Henna as quickly as he could. He had to bring her the young mother whose fate had worried her so. He pulled into the driveway of his house a few minutes later and let out a long sigh.

"Well, we're home."

Home. A word Rachel had not heard in a long time. Nor had she felt the concept of the word.

Home.

Henna. What would Henna be like? She quickly moved her hand to her hair and smoothed it down. She wiped her face and looked at Albert.

"Do I look okay? Is my face clean? I wish I had a brush. Do you have a brush?"

"You look just fine, child. He pulled out his clean hanky and wet the tip of it. He reached over and held Rachel's chin in his hand, gently he wiped a dark smudge from her left cheek.

"Henna, is not gonna look at the smudges on a face she's been longing to see. Don't forget this is the woman who has loved your child for the last year; no questions asked neither. Come on, let's go in."

With that, Albert moved out of the car quickly, went around to the passenger side, and opened the door for Rachel. He extended his hand and she took it and hand in hand they walked into the house.

Albert guided Rachel into the living room and sat her down on

the sofa. He motioned with a finger he would be right back then dis-
appeared into the next room. He closed the door to the bedroom and
stood looking at his sleeping wife.

What will all of this mean? Had he done right by stopping for
Rachel? What if she took Grace away? How will Henna take to this
young girl, the girl who left her baby on the side of the road not
knowing if it would even be found?

Albert stood there letting all these thoughts travel through his
mind. Not one rested in his heart and he took this as a good sign.
Henna stirred. He sat on the side of the bed and began to stroke her
back. He called her name softly. Henna stirred even more.

"Albert? You're late for work. Everything okay?" Henna spoke in a
sleepy voice.

"I'm not going in today. Henna, wake up darlin' I need you to
wake up."

Henna quickly opened her eyes and rolled over. "What's the matter? Where is Grace?" She tried to get out of bed but Albert held her
by the shoulders gently but firmly.

"Grace is just fine. I found her mama; actually, she found me."

Henna let out a gasp and stifled it with her hand. Her heart began
to pound and a single thought crossed her mind.

Grace. My baby, please don't let her take my baby.

Albert sensed her fear and pulled her into his arms.

"Baby, hush, it's not what you think. She's a child herself. She's
not come to take Grace. I brought her home so she can see that her
child's alive and in good hands. Hush, don't cry. You'll see what I
mean when you meet her. She's in the living room. Come on let's go.
Her name is Rachel. She can't be more than 14 or 15. And she's nothing but skin and bones."

Henna moved out of Albert's arms and to the closet to get her
robe. She followed Albert into the living room to see a frightened young
girl sitting on the edge of the sofa holding a picture in her hand.

It was the most recent picture of Grace that stood on the end
table. The girl was gently touching the picture with the tip of her
finger; a look of awe was on face.

"That was taken just two weeks ago. She's beautiful isn't she?"
Henna was the first to speak.

Rachel looked up at Henna and saw that like Albert this woman was looking at her with loving eyes. She stood up and handed the picture to Henna.

"She looks happy. She looks loved. Thank you."

Rachel began to sob and sat back down on the sofa.

Henna moved to her quickly, took her in her arms, and began to rock her.

"Oh, you poor baby. Hush, you poor child, it will be okay. Hush, Henna's here."

Henna held Rachel, stoking her back and rocking her gently. She let her quiet herself, knowing that all that pain inside was a great weight for someone so young. She knew this child's pain and let her continue to cry in her arms. They did not notice that Albert had slipped out of the room.

Although Rachel's tears had quieted when Albert returned, he still found them in the same embrace.

They didn't notice him until he spoke, "Rachel, this is Grace." Then more emphatically, "This is Grace."

He knelt down on the floor in front of Rachel and Henna. He balanced Grace on his knee with her facing away from him and toward the two on the sofa. Grace smiled at Rachel and reached her arms out to her.

Rachel looked at the child in front of her and wasn't sure what to do. She was afraid to touch her.

"Go on, honey, hold her." Henna encouraged the young mother to reach for her child.

"I can't. I'm afraid. I shouldn't touch her, not yet. I might hurt her. What if I hurt her?" Rachel spoke her fears out loud.

"You won't hurt her. She's not a china doll. She's sturdy and pretty strong, aren't you baby?" Albert nuzzled Grace in the back and she giggled out loud.

The sound took Rachel back and she flinched. Henna saw her fear and reached for Grace. She sat her on her lap and put her arms about her, she rested her face a long side of the baby's.

"She's a delight, Rachel, a pure delight. Don't be afraid. But if you want to wait, then you wait. We don't need to rush things unless you have somewhere to go? Is someone waiting for you somewhere?"

Henna knew the answer as she asked the question but stayed quiet while Rachel spoke.

"No. No one's waiting anywhere for me, I... I really don't have anywhere to go. I mean, I don't know where to go."

Albert took her hand but looked at Henna, "Why does she have to go anywhere? You don't have to leave just yet, Rachel. You need time to get to know your child. Isn't that right Henna?"

Henna nodded.

"That's right. You can stay here with us as long as you need to, Rachel. We have plenty of room in this house and in our hearts. Now put that thought of leavin' right out of your mind. You look like you could use a nice, hot shower and a good breakfast. Albert, take Grace into the kitchen and give her some juice. I'll show Rachel the bathroom and her room."

She handed Grace over to Albert, stood up, took Rachel by the hand, and led her down the hall. She kept right on talking, not waiting for Rachel to put up any resistance. Albert lifted Grace into the air and sang, "I got joy, joy, joy, joy, down in my heart." His notes could be heard behind the swinging door that separated the living room and the kitchen.

"Here's a clean towel and washcloth, honey, and I'll look in the closet for something for you to wear, unless you've got something in your pillow case that will do."

While Rachel began her shower a room away, Henna reached in the case and moved her hand about.

Henna's hand found the picture and pulled it out. She saw the faces of two children, obviously sisters. Although the young one was blond and Rachel, the older child, was darker, Henna could see by their faces how much the two loved one another.

She studied the picture, wondering what had become of the younger child. She replaced the picture and looked for something for Rachel to put on. She pulled out a pair of ragged jeans and another tee shirt. She put them to the smell test. They would do, for now. A shopping trip was in order.

The shower water stopped and Rachel pulled the curtain back just enough to let her face show. Henna shook out a bath towel and held it out for Rachel to step into and when she turned around her bony figure made Henna cringe.

A large, painful-looking bruise stood out on left side of Rachel's back. Henna remained silent, holding back shock and outrage. She wrapped the towel snugly around the girl and pulled her close.

"Who hurt you, child?"

When no response came, she reassured the girl that no had the right to do so. She put her face next to Rachel's and kissed her softly.

"And rest assured, no one but no one will ever leave a mark on you again. Not as long as Albert and I are around."

She turned Rachel around so that the two were facing one another. She took the young girl's face in her hands and wiped away fresh tears, then pulled her into her arms.

Her thoughts traveled back to the day she had first held Grace and had wondered where the mother of this newborn child was and how could she have left her on the side of the road as she had done.

Henna had her answer now. The child she was holding had done the only thing she knew to do. Henna tears mixed in the wetness of Rachel's newly washed hair.

"Come on baby, get dressed, we've got a breakfast to put in our stomachs. And goodness knows what mischief those two have gotten into. See you in a minute."

Henna gave Rachel a sound kiss on her cheek and left her alone to dress in private.

Henna entered the kitchen to the smell of coffee and toast.

"You want some bacon, honey?" Albert had put Grace on the floor and had begun to fix breakfast. The only thing Henna could see of Grace was her little bottom sticking out of the cabinet that held the pots and pans. Several had already made their way out and were scattered about the baby's feet.

"Bacon's fine. I'm gonna make some pancakes to go along with those eggs. Believe you me, that child needs some beefin' up — she's nothing but skin and bones. And someone's been badly mistreating her. She has a big bruise on her back that must have hurt plenty. You wouldn't treat a dog like that child's been treated."

Albert's eyes welled up. Rachel had told him about the foster home but had left out the part about being beaten.

"That poor girl has been through a really rough life, Henna. Her real Momma killed her little sister and is in prison because of it. Rachel writes to her, begging her to let her come and visit. The child has forgiven her but the woman still won't see her."

Henna thought about the picture in the pillowcase. The two children, the small blond child must have been Rachel's sister. A sharp pain pierced Henna heart. How could someone kill such a beautiful little child?

Rachel stood in the opening of the entrance to the kitchen from the hallway taking in what she was seeing. She didn't want to interrupt for fear of breaking something that look fragile to her unknowing eyes. Henna spotted her as she turned toward the refrigerator.

"Well, you look nice and fresh doesn't she Albert? Come here, honey. Sit down over here." She pulled a chair out for Rachel to sit in. It was right next to hers and Grace's highchair.

"Would you like me to help?" Rachel offered.

"No, sweetie, not this morning, you just sit yourself down and let someone else take care of you for a change."

Henna walked over, took Rachel by the shoulder, and guided her into the chair. She gave her a gentle hug before releasing her hold.

"Albert, put Grace in her chair and give her a handful of Cheerios in her Pooh Bowl."

Albert swooped up Grace, kissed her belly making her laugh and set her in the highchair next to Rachel. As he set her filled Pooh bowl in front of her, he winked at Rachel.

"Now don't let Rachel have any of these, Grace."

Using two tiny fingers, Grace delicately picked up a single piece of cereal, and held it out to Rachel. Rachel opened her hand, received the gift, and then put it into her mouth with a smile.

"She's pretty smart isn't she?"

Albert laughed, "Smart, honey? You don't know the half of it. Why this child, your child I might add, is the brightest baby I have ever laid eyes on. And I have three grown of my own and seven grandkids."

Henna put the plate of pancakes down in the center of the table and joined in.

"Albert likes to think he taught her all she knows but I know differently, now don't I, darlin'?"

Albert put one big arm around Henna and pulled her to him. He kissed her soundly on the cheek.

"Now you went and did it woman, you let out our big secret. No one is supposed to know what a smart man you're married to."

Grace clapped her hands together and demanded, "Up, Up."

She raised her arms toward Henna and Albert who readily picked her up to join their embrace. Rachel sat quietly absorbing all that she was seeing and feeling in this magical room, this simple kitchen, in the home of what appeared to be two simple people.

Tears filled her eyes and she covered her face to hide them. Albert spotted her and turned Henna to see her as well. She moved from Albert and Grace to Rachel and knelt near her chair. She gently pulled Rachel's hands away from her face.

"You don't ever have to hide your tears, darlin' — not ever. I can feel that you have so much pain inside. Albert and I will help you with that as best we can. And if that means you crying your eyes out when you need to then you go right ahead and cry. We will hold you if you let us and wipe away your tears. But I warn you, Albert is such a big cry baby that he'll join in every chance he can get."

Henna's words brought a smile to Rachel's lips. Henna took her hand and wiped away the tears on both of her cheeks. She held the young girl's face in her hands. Rachel looked at her and then at Albert.

"These are glad tears. Glad that you didn't let Grace die all alone on the side of the road. Glad that you both love her so much. And glad that you both seem to love each other so very much. I can feel it in your hands."

And with that, she took her own and placed them on top of Henna's own.

"Your hands are full of love. And you touch Grace with those hands. I'm really glad of that."

Albert let out a loud hoot.

"Honey, after a week in this house you're gonna be oozing love from the two — no, make it the 16 of us. Just wait to you meet the rest of the family."

Rachel could not remember a heartier breakfast than the one that followed. She hardly took her eyes off of Grace and Grace returned her look with a loving smile and an occasional Cheerio.

The day passed quickly with phone calls from the kids, who were each told of Rachel but encouraged to wait until morning to visit to give her a day to settle in. That evening when it was time to get Grace ready for bed Henna asked if Rachel wanted to help.

"Really, sweetie, she would love for you to give her bath."

"I know I had her — I mean, gave birth to her and all — but I'm not her Mom. You are. You know what, Henna? I only carried her, but you and Albert gave her a life. I could never have done that. Not the way you have. It's hard to explain, but when I look at her, I feel so strange. I can't quite say the right words yet but I love her, but I don't know in what way. I don't feel like her Mom — more like her sister. Is that wrong, Henna?"

"No, child, there's nothing wrong with anything you're feeling. Why you're only 14, how can you possibly know what being a mother feels like? Listen, Rachel you just go on feeling just how you're feeling. Albert and I aren't going anywhere. As long as there is mothering and fathering to do we'll do it. And that, my darlin', includes you. If you don't mind that is?"

Rachel felt more tears coming on.

Mind? Who would mind getting love from the likes of Henna and Albert, two loving people who took perfect strangers into their home and into their hearts without such much as a moment's hesitation.

How could Rachel mind being invited to spend a few days with them?

She couldn't even dream about living there for good. No. That would be too much, too big to think about.

"I wouldn't mind at all," she answered in a quiet voice then repeated the reply so as to make it more secure in her mind and heart.

"I wouldn't mind at all, Henna."

Henna sent Rachel into the living room to Albert while she got Grace bathed and into her pajamas.

Rachel found Albert sitting on the sofa with a large photo album on his lap. He glanced up, smiling and invited her to join him.

"Come on over here honey, take a look at the rest of the family."

Rachel took a seat next to Albert and saw what was making him smile from ear to ear. Picture after picture of faces smiling up at him that were no doubt his children and their families.

Birthdays and holidays, family dinners, fishing trips, the settings were endless. As Albert continued flipping through the pages of photos when he got to the more recent he stopped. He rested a finger on one of Henna holding a new baby.

"And this, Rachel, is Grace. This was taken just a few days after I found her. She's a beauty isn't she?"

'Rachel found herself reaching for the photo, hoping it would come loose from the book. It wouldn't, so she moved closer to Albert and let her fingers trace the image of the baby.

She'd lived! She didn't die alone on the side of the road. How grateful Rachel was that this big man sitting next to her had found the baby. Such terrible things could have happened and yet God had Albert find her. A tear trickled down her face on to the plastic covering.

"Would you like to keep this one? I know Henna wouldn't mind at all."

Albert began to lift the plastic and Rachel put her hand on his and stopped his motion.

"No. Don't. I want it left right here where it belongs. If I take it, there will be an empty space and that's no good. No, Grace needs to stay right here with the family who found her and loves her. I can look at it again, right? You don't think Henna would mind do you?"

"Not one bit. You can take this album out anytime you want to — and, look here." He began turning the pages and more and more picture of Grace appeared.

They were in chronological order so Rachel could see how she looked from birth to the most recent one taken only two weeks before. She was amazed at the smile on the baby and the look of love on the faces of those who surrounded her. There was one of all children; Grace was in the middle and in her lap was an even younger child.

"Are these your grandchildren?"

"Yes, and that little guy in Grace's lap is Jeffrey, the newest addition to the family. He's a cutie pie, ain't he? His Momma almost died giving birth to him. You wouldn't know it look at him now though would you? Yep, these are all our grandbabies. You can tell I'm a bit proud, huh?"

He gave Rachel a playful nudge and she shyly smiled back at him.

"Why, look at you. You've got one pretty smile. You think we'll get to see more of it once you get settled in?"

"I think we'll see as much of her smile as she feels comfortable in showing. Isn't that right, Rachel?" Henna walked in the living room holding Grace.

"This little lady is ready to say good night to one and all, aren't you, sweetie?"

She set Grace down and within seconds, the child was in Albert's arms. Her small arms wrapped around his thick neck and she buried her face next to his. Rachel sat back taking it all in, her eyes widening in the wonderment of the love she was seeing and feeling.

"You smell good enough to eat."

Albert lifted Grace into the air and nuzzled her belly. She let out peals of baby laughter that would delight anyone in earshot. He lifted her upright and stood her on his knees.

"Okay, little lady I think it's time for our story. Give Rachel a kiss goodnight so we can begin our nightly ritual.

He leaned her small body toward Rachel who sat upright not sure of what to do. As Grace moved close, her clean baby scent filled her up and as the soft tiny lips touched her cheek, Rachel had all she could do not to cry again. The softness of Grace reminded her suddenly of Stephi. Albert sensing something let Grace finish her kiss, stood up and hoisted Grace on his shoulders. "Nighty-night everyone."

Henna reached up and Albert stooped down so that she could plant a soundly kiss on Grace's cheek.

"Sweet dreams, lovey. Now, Albert when she's asleep let her be. You don't have to stand there and watch over her for another hour."

Albert and Grace marched off to her room leaving Rachel and Henna alone. Henna kept a glance on her newest child and wondered what pain was passing through her now.

"You want to talk about it, honey? I'll listen if you want to talk."

She sat down next to Rachel, put a hand on the slight girl's back, and began to rub it gently.

"Most times hurt can feel a lot less hurting if you share some with someone who's willing to share it. I'm here honey, and I'll take any hurt you want to give away."

Henna's hand felt Rachel's back tighten then give way. The floodgates of ache opened again as Rachel told Henna how she tried her best to take of care of her little sister, how she'd tried desperately to protect her from her mother and her mother's boyfriends, how she used to deal with the social workers, make sure that they had food, and clean things to wear.

And then she told her how it was only right before Stephi died that she remembered having Grace. She forgot until that moment that she had given birth; it came back like a really bad and scary dream.

After she remembered, all she worried about was that she had killed her baby by leaving her on the side of the highway. She didn't mean to do it she just couldn't take care of another baby.

Then she recounted the night Stephi died. Henna could picture the tragic night clearly, as Rachel spoke of holding her and wiping the blood away from her little sister's face. She could hear her voice as she sang Stephi a final lullaby. She could feel the young girl's pain as she recalled watching the EMT wheel her sister's body out of the apartment.

When the last words were out, Rachel's shoulders heaved with a deep sob escaping from her body. Henna pulled her into her arms and held her tightly, rocking her gently back and forth. She reached into her own heart, pulled out strength, and issued it Rachel.

She reached into Rachel's ache and gathered it up from inside out, then put it in her own heart knowing she had the years to deal with such grief. For no child should ever have to know what this child knew all too well.

As she continued to rock her, she began to hum and slowly the ache left the child and she felt Rachel's body relax. She rocked and sang softly to the child letting her own tears fall. She didn't try to brush them away nor worry that it would reveal her weak. She closed her eyes, held Rachel and the rocking soothed them both.

"Honey, honey..."

Albert was shaking her ever so softly.

"Henna, darlin' she's asleep." He took his hand and wiped his wife's face. The tears had streaked her cheeks.

"Looks like she opened up to you and you let it all fall right into your heart. God bless you, Henna, and how He blessed me for marrying you."

"Shush, you'll wake her. Go in the bedroom and turn back her covers. Make sure you leave the night light on for her. Then come back and carry her to bed."

Albert did as instructed in the bedroom and then returned to the living room and without any effort, lifted Rachel into his arms and followed Henna into the bedroom.

He laid her down gently then left the room while Henna got the sleeping girl into a nightgown. He returned with a stuffed animal that belonged to Grace and placed it in Rachel's arms, smiling as she pulled it in close.

The two pulled up the covers and tucked them snugly around their newly found child. Henna joined Albert, leaned back into his arms and rested her head against Albert's chest. The two just stood in silent thanksgiving that Rachel had found her way to them. After a while, Henna spoke softly.

"You know, Albert, the morning you placed Grace in my arms I wondered what kind of mother could leave her baby out to die on the side of the road. I wondered how much hurt inside could make her think that was the only thing to do.

"After hearing of her life, there was no question — Even if our Grace had died, this child could not bear one more weight on her small shoulders. I don't think I've ever met anyone so young with such strength Albert. We have a lot to learn from this child. She will be a gift to us."

Albert kissed Henna's cheek and swayed slightly. He let his lips rest on Henna's ear and whispered softly.

"She's here for the same reason Grace is here and that's because God Himself led her to our home. Come on, sweetie, let's call it a night."

Henna removed his arms and bent over Rachel, brushed the hair from her face and gently kissed her forehead. Albert followed suit pulling the covers up to her chin; one last tucking in for the night. Then the two quietly left the room leaving the door opened just a tad.

Although the night was still young, both were spent, so Albert and Henna settled in one another arms in bed. Each slept a bit more peacefully knowing that the proverbial "other shoe" that had just fallen had landed softly indeed.

GYADA

*T*he desert moon, full and luminous, brightened all that was above and below. Its light captured Gyada as she stirred the fire with a smile on her face. She looked up and spoke without opening her mouth.

"Thank you for watching and guiding her to her child; she is safe. The two you chose will protect her and share their love with her. I have yet to hear my name whispered by the little one. When will the lesson begin?

"*Soon.*"

She continued to communicate with her thoughts. "The Changes move more quickly now."

"The time is known, Gyada. Do not worry about that which is planned; just listen with your heart. Remember, we choose well."

Gyada's outward smile resonated within her as well. The exchange ended. The moon continued to spread its light and the woman continued to stir her fire.

A new glow appeared joining the others, this one from Gyada's heart. She knew that when the time came she would have the right words to say to Grace.

She was anxious to begin.

A New Beginning

The next few days each felt like glorious Christmas mornings, as each family was introduced to Rachel.

On Sunday, the entire clan gathered around the table making her feel welcomed, wanted, and loved. As all hands joined for a prayer of thanksgiving Albert and Henna stood on either side of Rachel each holding on tightly to a hand.

Albert began, "Once again, dear Lord, we are thankful for all that you continue to provide for us. You watch over us, your children, with a most tender and generous love. Continue to guide us as we make our way on this earth; help us to serve you by serving yours. Lord, thank you for leading Rachel home. Although we did not birth her, she is indeed one of our own. Amen."

All stood silently in prayerful thanksgiving not wanting to break the bond that gave each one of them strength. All adults present knew the world was now a sad and frightening place in which to live.

War, hunger, violence and natural disasters now commonplace; not one of those present could imagine a child of 14 on her own to face such a world.

So, it did not come as a surprise to any of those gathered that Henna and Albert would welcome Rachel permanently into their home and into their hearts, anyone save Rachel. The young girl looked up and searched their eyes for meaning; her mind could not take in what her longing heart already understood. She could not speak.

True to form, Albert broke the silence.

"Well, what do you think, Rachel? Do you think you could make a home here? Henna and I...well, as you see we live a simple life, but if you want, we want to share it with you."

Henna added her own thoughts.

"I know I'm not your Mama honey, but I will love you as though you were my own, just like Grace. Grace is here because of you, so, I can only imagine that you are here because of her. As far as Albert and I can see this was planned by someone looking down from above. What do you say darlin', will you stay for good?"

Rachel's "Yes" was whispered into Henna's bosom as she threw her arms around her. Albert gathered them both in and the rest of the family cheered and clapped loudly for joy.

Susie, holding hands with Ruth, raised her voice especially loud knowing, the lesser outcome that may well have occurred.

"Praise God, another woman in the house! A shopping trip! Mama, we need to get this child to the mall."

The meal now took precedence; but for the most part Rachel sat back in awe taking in her newfound family.

Days passed in to weeks and since no one came looking for her, Henna, and Albert did for Rachel as they did for Grace and went on about their life.

As far the foster care system, Rachel was a runaway, one of the thousands who fled broken homes each year; nobody seemed to be trying to find her.

Rachel was smart enough to have kept copies of all her records, so come Fall, her school registration went without a hitch.

Well, the records did require a little doctoring and an additional letter of adoption that came by way of a trusted friend of Al Jr. but all in all, no one raised an eyebrow when Henna took Rachel to register for the ninth grade at the local junior high school.

The secretary was thrilled to see a parent who actually asked for the PTA meeting schedule and also inquired about how she and her husband might volunteer at the school.

"Here you go. The first meeting is next Wednesday evening at seven. They usually hand out lists of committees that are in need of more hands. They'll be thrilled to hear that you have four to offer!"

Rachel, here is your class schedule and a copy for your —"

"Mother."

Henna finished the woman's sentence with ease and with a smile. Rachel let out a gentle sigh as the corners of her mouth turned up into a slight smile, which grew bigger from a kiss that Henna planted on her cheek.

"Mother" she repeated in a whisper.

School began the next day and both Henna and Albert were impressed with Rachel's attitude toward her studies. In spite of all the difficulties of her young life she had done well in school. Now with the chance to be just a young girl in the ninth grade, she began to soar.

Test after test reflected a perfect score, assignments, and homework done resulting in nothing less than "A" work.

At the parent-teacher meeting two months into the school year, there was nothing but praise and all commented on her constant willingness to help others in class who struggled. Then she got her Iowa tests results, scoring on the twelfth grade level in all areas. Henna and Albert sat back in amazement as Rachel's advisor shared the news.

"We would like you to consider letting her take a few upper-class courses, especially in math and science," said Miss Meriwether. "Rachel's teachers have given her advanced work already and she continues to pull "A's" in work that is beyond her academic year.

"With your permission, we would like to place her in Calculus and Chemistry II. We could let her sit in on a class to make sure she was comfortable socially and if so allow her to finish the year in those courses.

"Over the summer, if she is interested, Yale offers classes to high school students of her caliber, in many disciplines and for which college credits are given. If Rachel continues at this rate, she will be offered numerous scholarships and at some very prestigious schools, I might add. Students like Rachel don't come along too often."

Speechless and moved to tears, Henna's only thoughts were, *If only you knew the life, this child has endured. Imagine where she would be today if it had begun with love.*

Albert spoke for them both.

"If this is something Rachel wants and can handle then we will gladly give our permission. I'm sure you're all aware that we're not her natural parents, and her life was — well, to say it was hard does not do her justice.

"My, our, only concern will be the amount of pressure put on her. This child does not need anything that puts her under more pressure. But I know she is one bright girl and shared with us her desire to be a doctor one day, so if this speeds up that process and she's for it, then so our we. Do you agree, Henna? Did I say it alright?"

"You said it just fine, Albert. And yes, I agree. If Rachel thinks she can handle all of this then we will do all we can to help her."

The meeting ended with a great deal of enthusiasm and laughter as one of the faculty placed a bet that Rachel would be sporting a stethoscope before he learned basics of Word 2000.

Henna and Albert smiled, not caring that neither had a clue that the rest of the intellectual world would find this humorous. For their world revolved around the day to day of a simple life where what mattered most was sharing their hearts and home with those they loved.

As Rachel devoured her new studies the year and summer flew by, come fall she was placed in the 12th grade. She earned nine college credits over the summer and was going to carry six more during the fall semester. Her ability to comprehend all she was given amazed teachers at both the high school and the University. Her appetite for knowledge was never satiated.

Grace too began her lessons with an eager teacher. However, hers was not seen by anyone, not even Grace. When alone in her room she sat quietly with her eyes closed, nodding her head ever so slightly. The lessons had begun only months before when two-year-old Grace whispered from her heart the name "Gyada" repeating it over and over until a voice returned her call.

"I am with you. You will not see me, yet, but when you call I will answer."

The voice heard within the child's heart brought a smile to her lips. She was thirsty but hasn't known for what — until now. When Gyada answered her call, her thirst was quenched, but only for a while, for she knew the well was deep and there was much to drink in.

And so it was a time of learning for both Rachel and Grace. The older girl unknowingly readied herself to heal the physical wounds of her broken brethren, the younger one prepared to heal and make ready their hearts for the time to come.

SEPTEMBER 11TH, 2001
4:30 AM

I don't know what's wrong with her, something has the child upset."

Henna held a distraught Grace in her arms, walking back and forth in the living room as a concerned Albert walked right next to her.

"Is she teething? Maybe it's her two-year molars. Remember Susie? She kept us up for nights on end till they came in."

"No, it doesn't seem physical, it's like she's worried, Albert; worried about something. You can see she's not crying in pain, but something big is troubling this little child."

"Should we take her to the doctor? Maybe he'll see something we can't."

"I already called him. But she doesn't have fever, and there's no swelling or redness anywhere. I'm telling you Albert, her heart is sad, she's grieving about something."

Henna held Grace close and whispered to her softly, "Oh, precious, let your mama take it from you. I can't bear to see you suffer so."

"I'll call in to work and let them know I won't be in. You want me to fix us some coffee? It looks like we're all up for the day."

He motioned to Rachel who stood in the doorway.

"Is she okay? You want me to hold her for a while?"

Grace lifted her head and stretched out her arms to Rachel who ran to Henna's side. She lifted the child into her arms and sat down on the sofa. Grace looked into Rachel's eyes then let out a long mournful sigh, followed by silent tears that flowed down her small cheeks. The family sat awaiting a call back from the doctor, who would examine the child later that morning but would find nothing physically wrong.

It was not until 8:55 that morning of September 11th, 2001 that the reasons for the child's grief became apparent, however, not to her immediate family, but to the one who waited patiently in the desert of Cibola, New Mexico. Only Gyada knew why the child was filled with such sorrow and there was nothing, nor anyone that could give her comfort.

*D*o you think she'll want to see me now? So much time has passed and yet she still doesn't answer my letters."

Rachel questioned Henna about her mother, who remained in prison in Niantic.

Henna responded, but paused before her final words were out.

"It's hard to say, sweetie. I can only imagine what she must be feeling. No, I really can't say I would know the amount of guilt I would heap on myself after killing my own child. Maybe my letter, if she reads it, will put her at ease.

"I explained that you only want to see her, to let her know that you understand that it was the drugs not her that took your sister's life. Well, no matter what the response, if there is one this time, I and all the rest of the family will be right here by your side, you can count on that for sure."

She put her arms around the girl and pulled her close. At 17, Rachel was a beautiful young woman who took things in stride but tended to be more on the serious side. Physically, she stood with straight shoulders and trim body that supported her 5-foot, 7-inch frame.

Her auburn hair was thick and wavy and hung just past her shoulders. Her deep blue eyes stood out in contrast with her creamy white skin.

When she smiled the room lit up. Her infectious laughter came easily when Albert began his antics, or when Grace was the center of attention for behaving like many other three–year-olds.

"Maybe a call would help. In all this time, I've never called; I've been too afraid that she wouldn't speak to me. Do you think she thinks that I don't love her anymore, Henna?"

"I think it's more about her loving herself, honey. I'm sure if she reads your letter and finds out that you're doing really well, that maybe she'll start to soften a bit on her self.

"We mothers, no matter how wicked or harsh, only want to see our children do better than we did in life. A lot can't even breathe those words out loud.

"Goodness knows your Mama had a tough life, probably as tough as you had, that's why she couldn't stop herself from using the drugs and causing you such suffering.

"What do you know about her life? Her mother and father? There's the key, darlin', children pass on what they know, what they learn when they're little.

"Oh, people can change the course all right, but that takes a mighty courageous and determined person to succeed and not everyone can do it, and most don't. That's why were in such a sorry state in our world.

"There's so many wounded people out there that I can only image things are twice as bad as it seems, because folks don't always share what's going on in their lives."

Rachel confirmed Henna's previous thought.

"I never told anyone what went on at home — not my teachers at school or neighbors, not anyone. I was too afraid that my mother would just get angrier at me and take it out on Stephi."

The mentioning of her little sister caused her to lower her chin and cover her face. Henna pulled her close once again.

"You have every right in the world to feel sad about what happened to your sister, but no right to accept blame for what your mother did. That I won't let you do.

"Now, you listen to me, Rachel, no one could have done a better job of caring for Stephi for the six years that precious child had on Earth. Why, you were a baby yourself caring for a newborn.

"Goodness child, my children were bright when they were little, but I can't imagine that one of them would be able to handle doing such a thing. Now, let's wipe these tears, take ourselves into the backyard, and persuade Albert to take us all for ice cream. Not that we need to do much persuading of course but we both know he'll put up a good show about watching his weight."

The two women went out the back door to join the others. However, Henna had already determined she would place a phone call to the women's prison soon, if no letter came from Rachel's mother.

Enough is enough, it was time for mending and she knew she had just the words to say to make that begin to happen.

As it turned out, she wouldn't need to call, for two days later, a letter arrived for Rachel.

It was the first communication between mother and child since that horrible night nearly four years earlier. Henna held the envelope in her hand, wishing she could read it before Rachel, but knowing she had no right to do so. Rachel however, placed it back into her hands asking her to do just that.

"I'm too afraid, Henna. Would you, please read it before me? I'll go sit on the porch and wait."

Before Henna could utter a word, Rachel was out the front door. She sat at the kitchen table and slowly and carefully opened the envelope, then removed the single page letter that contained this simple message:

Dear Rachel,

I don't know how to say I'm sorry big enough or loud enough to make it count for what I did. But I want you to know, that I am sorry and that I can only imagine how much you hate me for killing Stephi. I hope someday you will forgive me, but I know that I will never forgive myself. I have never opened one of your letters because I was too afraid of what you would say to me. I don't even know if you're going to get this but the guard told me that they had your address from your last letter and that they would address for me. I love you Rachel and I am sorry.

Love, Mommy

Henna wiped her tears and blew her nose before folding the letter and placing it back into the envelope. She stood and braced herself for the flood of emotion she knew would be pour out when Rachel read these few simple words.

She kept faith, however, that the words "I'm sorry" could move mountains and this indeed would lift a huge burden from the young woman's heart.

She opened the screen door and joined Rachel, who sat with her arms resting on her knees, and her head down taking up a small space on the front steps of the house.

Rachel turned and looked up when she heard the screen door open. Henna sat down next to her putting the letter into her trembling hands then placed her arm around Rachel's shoulders. It only took a few moments for her to read her mother's note and when she lowered it into her lap, she buried her face into Henna waiting arms.

"She loves you, child, she's still so ashamed and sad over what she did, but it's a start honey, it's a start. Maybe if you write her back she'll open it this time. Maybe we can call and see if she'll let us visit.

"We'll get Susie and Ruth and Betty to go along. Yes, that's what we'll do, we women we'll go help another who but the grace of God could be one of us. What do you say? I don't think she'll turn us away, not if we all go there together, and offer her only love and understanding."

"Would you do that for me? How come you don't hate her, or look down on her for what she did, using drugs and all and — what she did to Stephi?

Henna took Rachel's face into her hands.

"Rachel, every child born is innocent and pure and in the likeness of the Creator, and capable of magnificent works, but if born into the lives of the wounded more wounds are made. We humans have made quite a mess of things and God knows, it's getting worse every moment. The only thing we have to offer your mother is our love, if she'll take it. There's no guarantee that will be the case."

"Why didn't I turn out like her? When I was in some of the foster homes there were kids in there that were… Well, they were mean and angry. Some of them did things to make it worse. What will happen when they grow up if no one loves them?"

"More then likely the same thing that happened to them, but it doesn't have to be that way, I think that there's just too many wounded in the world and not as many to heal. And as far as you go, you are meant for greatness, not in money or fame, but you are here for many, just like your, our, precious Grace. You had to know the suffering in order to know the pain of many and you will use that knowledge in ways we can't even begin to see at this moment."

"Should we bring Grace with us, if we go?"

"Well, I'm not sure on that. Maybe we should have a meeting with the girls and Albert and see what they think. My mind is a bit over-whelmed right this moment, but we'll do the right thing, no matter which way we go. Of course we have to call and see if she is willing to let us come."

"Maybe if we only let her know that I will be coming... then maybe she'll say yes. I'm going to write her back right away and tell her I forgive her and that I want to see her – soon."

Rachel hugged Henna tightly then jumped up and raced into the house to respond to her mother's letter. She kept her words simple but made in clear that she loved and forgave her a long time ago and wanted to see her badly.

She was going to come for a visit the following weekend and hoped that when she got there she would see her. She addressed and stamped the letter, then she and Henna drove to the post office to mail it.

Before the weekend visit, the family met and decided that Grace would not go this time. Then Henna placed a call to the corrections facility to make sure it would be permissible for them all to visit all at once, explaining the situation to the understanding woman on the phone who readily agreed, then added the names to the visitors list. Henna let out a deep sigh as she replaced the phone receiver on the hook. She was venturing into waters that she was not familiar with at all.

In her wildest dreams, she had never thought she would be visit-ing a woman imprisoned for killing her own child, then almost as sad, refusing to see the only one remaining for four years. The amount of pain that poor soul must be in — *Why, I can't even imagine,* she thought to herself.

Saturday came and they made the one-hour ride to the women's prison without knowing for sure of the outcome of the visit.

Whatever it was, strong and loving women who would stay would surround Rachel by her side. As they piled out of the car, they linked arms and with Rachel in the center walked the short distance to the entrance of the facility.

All passed through the security gates, metal detectors, reclaimed their purses that were properly examined then sat as instructed on a nearby bench awaiting their turn to be called. Rachel stood and started to pace in front of the others. When she passed by Henna for the third time, Henna, reached for her hand and pulled her into her lap.

"You're going to walk a path into the floor. She'll see you, I believe with all my heart she will want to see you."

Susie, sitting next to Henna, took Rachel's other hand, kissed it and put it to her cheek.

"You are so courageous and brave, I'm so proud of you that I could just burst."

On the last of her words, a female guard called out for them to come forward. The five women followed the guard through yet another steel door, into a room that had six metal picnic tables and benches secured to the ground.

Seated at one, with her back to them was a thin, small-boned woman whom they imagined was Rachel's mother Ellie. The guard nodded her head in the direction of the woman then stayed put near the door allowing the women to go to the table on their own.

They walked together, then Rachel stopped them, motioning she would go the remaining steps alone. Rachel walked slowly to her mother and touched her shoulder.

"Mom?"

Rachel's voice was barely a whisper. Ellie turned around in her direction and gave the faintest of gasps.

"Rachel? Oh, my God, Rachel, look at you, you're here...you came."

Ellie stood and extended her arm to reach out and touch Rachel's hair, then her face.

"You're beautiful, look at you."

Rachel tenderly took her mother's hand into both of her own and kissed it, causing Ellie to crumble into a heap back on the bench. Rachel immediately went to her, and kneeling in front of her, threw her arms around her.

"Oh Mommy, I missed you. I wanted to see you, and tell you that it was all right, that I understood what happened. I know it was not you that night. I know you were sick, that you loved Stephi and me as much as you could."

Ellie responded in between her sobs of anguish.

"I'm so sorry, so sorry... you don't know how each and every day I think about what I did and wish with everything inside of me to take that night back. I wish I could take all of what I did... to you back. How can I ever expect you to forgive me?"

"But I do, Mom — I forgave you a long time ago. I had to because not forgiving took up too much space in my heart and made me really sad.

"It made me feel better to forgive you and hope that one day we could be together again or at least that you might let me come to visit you sometime. What you did was not who you really are. I learned that we do things because we don't know any better. We all do things that we don't plan on doing."

Ellie could not yet accept her daughter's forgiveness.

"But I should've let them keep you in foster care the first time, and then you wouldn't have had to go through what you did that night."

"Mommy, then I wouldn't have gotten to know Stephi. I loved her. I loved her so much. I miss her, but I know she's okay. I know she's with me every day, like an angel, she's with me everywhere I go."

Rachel brushed her mother's tears from her face then did the same with her own.

Henna came up behind her and offered her tissues, Ellie looked up and gave her a trembling smile and mouthed the words thank you. Rachel stood and raised her mother up with her.

"I want you to meet my... family, Mom. They took me in three years ago and treat me like one of their own. I wouldn't be here today, if it weren't for them."

She took Henna by the hand and held it tightly then said with much pride.

"This is Henna, and that's Susie, Ruth, and Betty; everyone this is my Mom, Ellie."

Within seconds, the four women encircled the other two; love was the only energy that flowed out of them.

The rest of the visit flew by and the group shared much information. Ellie was overjoyed at Rachel's success at school and laughed at all the antics of Albert and the men of the family.

Grace was not mentioned, for there was no way to explain her to Ellie.

Ellie shared that her sentence was 15 years for taking Stephi's life; she added that it did not matter because no sentence would be long enough to punish her enough for what she did.

The others sat quietly allowing her the dignity of righteous guilt, but offered her comfort through their touch.

When it came time to leave, the women traded hugs all around

and shed many more tears. Rachel made plans to visit again and promises of frequent letters.

As the women were escorted out of the room, Rachel made one
last dash back to hug her mother and whisper into her hair.

"I love you to pieces, Mommy."

She turned quickly and joined the others as they passed through
the steel door. When it clanged shut, she gave a shudder, buried her
head into Henna arms and wept.

Before they left, the guard returned and asked to speak with Henna
privately.

"Did she tell her? Did she tell her that she's dying — from AIDS?"

Henna put her hand to her mouth to silence the audible sigh of
sadness and replied simply, "No."

The guard went on, "I didn't think so. She doesn't want her girl to
feel sorry for her; she just wanted to make sure she knew that she was
sorry for what she had done. She's one sad lady, who got one raw deal
after the next...just like most of them in here."

Henna inquired quietly, "How much time does she have... Do
they know?"

"She's was sick before she got convicted, more than likely went
untreated for quite awhile so the disease had a chance to do a lot of
damage. She's up for a transfer to a medical facility when a bed opens
up. The place is in Massachusetts but it filled, they expect soon one
soon, but no one can say for sure. Do you want to know when it
happens? Should I tell Ellie that I told you? I don't honestly think that
she'll mind. She has no one, you know — not one visitor in all the
years she's been here."

To this Henna responded with much conviction, "You tell her
that I know. Tell her that now she has someone, no, not just someone... That she has a family, a family who will come and visit as often
as she will allow. And tell her that she doesn't ever have to worry about
her baby, because Rachel is loved and cared for just like she dreamed
about doing for her herself."

The guard, moved to tears, made one more request.

"Do you think you could tell her that yourself before you leave?
It's not exactly policy but, under the circumstances, I know it will be
okay."

Henna smiled and nodded "Yes," and the guard brought her back in to the visitor's room and returned in a few moments with Ellie. The two women sat at the nearest table and said nothing but held the gaze of each other's eyes.

Ellie spoke first.

"I couldn't tell her. Do you understand, I just couldn't tell her?"

"Well, from what I understand, your time... she's going to need to know before you pass, darling. You have to give her a chance to get used to seeing you again and then — losing you. She's really strong Ellie, stronger then most grown women and she won't be alone to handle things, you can count on that."

Ellie reached across the table for Henna hands and began to sob. Henna glanced up quickly to the guard who nodded yes, giving permission for her to sit beside the wounded Ellie.

"Shhh, sweet child. You won't face this alone either. You can count on that, too. I'm here baby, I'm here and you are never going to be alone again...even if your days are few, you are not going to be alone."

Henna held Ellie until the guard came up and tapped her on the shoulder indicating the rules had been broken long enough. When escorted out of the room once again, Henna embraced the guard, acknowledging her for her act of kindness.

"You are evidence that the heart of God lives."

Henna left the building and joined her family in the car, giving them the news of Ellie's true sentence. Susie began the dialogue.

"I knew the minute I saw her that she was seriously ill. I even suspected it was AIDS. Well, at least you can be assured that she's getting the required treatment. I mean the state is obligated by law to provide it."

To which Henna responded, "If she was taking it. Her shame and guilt over what she did won't allow that. She wanted the judge to give her a death sentence.

"She told me that he was only going to give her seven years because of the circumstances of the drugs and diagnosis of the AIDS, and begged for the 15 years, saying it was not nearly enough to pay for what she did or the suffering she heaped on Rachel."

Turning to Rachel now, she added.

"They think that she's only months away from dying. Goodness knows how people think they know the plans of God. Well no matter, I assured her that she would not face her time alone. She might have come into this world unwanted and shamefully regarded, but that is not how she's leaving it. You can bet on that, darlin' — once Albert hears of this, there will be no stopping him from making her last days more beautiful than you can imagine.

"In fact, I know I speak for my entire family — we have just grown by one. Goodness knows the corrections department doesn't know what has just fallen upon them."

The last statement evoked a laugh from all, even Rachel through her sorrow, knew that this family who had embraced her so openly upon first meeting, would do likewise for her mother.

And so it was just as Henna predicted, the entire family made regular visits and sent frequent letters to Ellie.

Henna began with a letter that quickly changed to phone calls and a visit to the department of corrections, then on to the Governor's office, petitioning for them to release Ellie into their care instead of being moved to the facility in Massachusetts.

The same benevolent friend who helped with Rachel's adoption papers moved a few mountains that resulted in an early release, given the statement from the judge's who relayed his intended sentence.

On June 13th, Ellie left the women's correctional center in a wheelchair and after being carefully lifted into the car by Albert, she made the hour's journey to her new and final home with Rachel and Henna at her side.

The entire family was there to greet her when the car pulled up to the house. Susie made ready the rented hospital bed that Albert had set up in the spare bedroom.

The room was anything but hospital-like for all the women in the family, both old and young saw to making it warm and cozy. Next to the bed was an overstuffed rocking chair that had once sat in Grace's room.

All that Ellie knew about Grace was she was taken in by the family when she was just an infant. This would be the first time meeting her and the other children of the brood.

This was something very different for the entire family. No one had ever lost someone close to them, and especially under these circumstances. But just like everything else, it was taken in stride, done with love and even a sense of humor.

Ten days passed and all was quiet; at three in the morning on the eleventh night, Ellie was resting as comfortably as possible having been medicated for pain an hour before by Susie, who was napping on the living room sofa.

Grace tiptoed into the room and stood at the side of the bed. She put her hand on Ellie's arm and stroked it gently causing the woman to open her eyes and whisper.

"I thought I was dreaming... I saw an angel...she looked just like you. It won't be long now, will it?"

The child spoke to her gently.

"No. Close your eyes Ellie, look, for Stephi. Do you see her? She's there, do you see her?"

Ellie's weakened voice was lifted with joy.

"Yes...she's over there."

She called to her child. "Stephi...she's smiling...She's waving for me to come."

Grace assured her with much love, "She's smiling because she's happy... she's waiting for you. Go to her, Ellie. Go on, it time for you to be at peace."

Ellie's entire body became aglow with a warm light that lifted from her body and became a mist that transcended above her. Grace gathered the light into her small hands then went to the open window, lifted her arms, and released the spirit of Ellie into the night whispering these words:

"Be at peace."

The door to the room was ajar and Albert stood quietly, watching the child. As Grace turned from the window, the two exchanged a loving smile.

More people than could be counted on — twenty sets of hands and feet — attended Ellie's funeral. Included among them was the guard from the prison who had put all of this into motion by one act of kindness.

PREPARATIONS

$\mathscr{C}$ome summer of 2005, things had changed greatly in the neighborhood where Albert and Henna lived, prompting additional worries of the times to come.

Rachel continued her accelerated academic path and was nearly finished with a degree in organic biology at Yale. She was admitted early into the University's Medical school with much anticipation of what she would contribute to the field of organic medicine.

Her professors were continually amazed at her intuitive ability to progress to the natural order of new discovery. She by-passed steps of accepted protocol in numerous analyses saving both time and money in the laboratory, of course the department chair was beyond pleased. On her own time, she began to tap into the natural healing elements of the human body. Her records were meticulously kept in her journals as well as in her mind.

When the two would spend time together, she shared her work with Grace. It did not matter that the child was only six.

There was nothing that Grace did not understand, as a matter of fact, she often would ask a question, knowingly, and that would lead Rachel to yet another discovery of the natural healing abilities possessed by women.

This was not to say that men were not equipped with such, but that women held a much higher degree of a natural means to diagnose and heal the physical, emotional and mental diseases of the human body.

She had identified the strain of DNA that held such information while working with blood samples from the family, as well as hundreds of additional slides from anonymous individuals.

She made two significant discoveries. The first was that in nearly 98 percent of the females studied there was a bend in the T that was elongated in a unique but extremely subtle manner that was not present in the males.

She did not discover this until the third pass through, and only after speaking with Grace who prodded her with this thought.

"The shape of what we think is so is not as clearly formed — women are bent with a natural inclination to nurture and to heal."

This was all that the student needed. Rachel's new quest was now to translate that information in to practical methods of instruction for women.

How can she teach them to tap into such incredible abilities? She knew immediately that would be an uphill battle and again sought direction from Grace who would be even more than just a source of information she would become the teacher. However, it was not yet time to do such and she explained that to Rachel.

"I need to tell you something you may find hard to understand. But first I must ask you, what do you remember of my birth?"

Rachel was taken back to a place that she had put aside for many years. She closed her eyes and was brought back to that night then spoke softly.

"I felt completely alone and afraid. After I had you, I was so angry and I raised my fists to the sky and screamed out that I could not take care of you."

"Do you remember what the sky looked like that night?"

Rachel sat still for a while and closing her eyes once again, she put herself back at the site of the birth. She lifted her head and looked up as she had that night; she stood and raised her arms to the sky. She quickly drew in her breath and turned to look at the child who was now standing beside her.

"There was a star — a brilliant star that suddenly appeared. It kept growing brighter by the second. I had never seen such a star... It was like, when..."

She stopped speaking and knelt down in front of the Grace.

"Was that for you? Was the star meant to let others know of your birth?"

Grace responded was a quiet and simple, "Yes."

Rachel sat back down and Grace joined her. The two sat in silence for quite sometime until Rachel raised the courage to ask, "Why me?"

"Because you were chosen long before, right from the beginning to be part of this moment in time."

"By whom?"

"By the one who created all."

"God? Why would he choose me?"

"Yes, God, but God is not a he or a she as you say. God is...how can I say this for you to understand? Do you see the tree over there? That is God. And the bird flying in the sky – that is God. And this rock and this one and that one over there... that is God. Beneath the rock and between the bark and root of the tree is God. All of this is God."

Then Grace placed her hand on Rachel's heart and smiled, "And most importantly, this is God."

"Why did they send you, at this time?"

"I am here as are you, Rachel, to teach humanity those very things. People around the world have journeyed far from this knowledge. Only a few throughout time have understood and, sadly, most people – people who should have known better — thought they were heretics or insane.

The world is going through a major change, an end of a time filled with much sadness. However, it is a better time that is coming, a joyous era where love will reign and peace abound. We have much to do, much preparation to put into place if we are to reach as many was told to me."

"How will we reach them? Won't we be looked at as insane or heretics?"

Grace could not help but let out a laugh, "Well, we're both still learning the answers to that and regarding how and what they will think of us...I can't even begin to say. But this time will be different from last; it will not end as it did before. For this time, as promised, she will triumph in the end."

"Who will triumph?"

"God, Goodness. I only use 'she' because that is the form that came to Earth, that still comes to Earth with words and promises of peace. Do you know of the events that took place in Fatima, Portugal in 1917? Or of the visits that began in 1981 in Medjugorie, Yugoslavia or in 1985 in Naju, Korea or in 1990 in Conyers, Georgia?

"The visits are countless and the message is always the same. Humanity must return to living the spirit of God that is in all. They run in fear from the knowledge that all are one with God. There is no distinction between the two. Religions of the world have created a schism between that which is God and that, which is human. There is no break — no separation, that which is God is human and that which is human is God. That is what we must teach them."

"Us? You mean you — don't you?"

Again, Grace smiled, "No, I mean — Us. You are learning things that can be taught and I can do things already that will attract attention to such. We're not quite ready yet to begin. I am still learning things from Gyada."

"Who is Gyada? And what is it that you are learning?"

Grace stood and walked a few steps from where she and Rachel were seated. She looked up into the sky and waited.

As she stood there, a white mist engulfed her and Rachel, who remained quite still, heard a low humming sound. Suddenly the mist lifted and Grace turned to her and spoke.

"Gyada is the one who has been waiting for a very long time for my birth. She lives high in the mountains of New Mexico. She speaks to me through her spirit — she shows me things from worlds away. She gives me the words to say to you to help you and soon to help the others to understand the plan of the Creator."

"Have you ever seen her?"

"Yes, but in a way I don't yet have the words to tell you, but soon I will take you there. Soon we will all go there. We have much to do before that journey but it will not be long I promise. I think we should be getting back or poor Henna will be worried about us."

"Do they know about you? That you're special?"

"Not exactly, but Albert knows in his heart, he was told the morning he found me. One day the whole family will be told. All of the family was chosen to be part of this time on earth.

"It wasn't a coincidence that you returned to the very spot a year later, the very spot that Albert had found me. There is no such thing as coincidence, Rachel. Is it is merely paths laid out more clearly that some choose to follow and some do not."

"How will you teach the others? Won't they question whom you are and doubt the truth of it?"

"Sadly, yes, but we'll begin with the easy ones... the family, they have gotten to know that I'm a bit different."

She giggled once again, stood and took Rachel's hands and pulled her to her feet.

"Come on, I'll race you to the car."

～ ～ ～ ～ ～ ～ ～ ～ ～ ～

Two years later Grace was to enter second grade at the local public school, and the lessons for the family began. Coincidentally, public schooling was no longer safe so the family began to home school the children, with all the adults sharing the teaching.

Soon it was apparent that Grace was as much the teacher as was the adult holding class for the day. The lesson was about sitting still and listening to the world around them. Or, as Grace pointed out, that it is at times more important to hear with one's heart that which cannot be heard by one's ears.

They ventured to Seaside Park and the entire group sat cross-legged on the sand looking out at the Sound without so much as a whisper between them.

They listened to and observed what was around them. The listened with complete attention to the waves gently lapping the shore and to the seagulls that dipped down and snatched a snail then soared up into the sky dropping their catch with a continued snapping against the wet sand.

They observed a dog playing fetch with his master, eagerly and repeatedly retrieving a tennis ball from the water, each time being rewarded with a "Good boy!" followed by, "Go it get, boy!"

They could hear his paws sink slightly into the sand spraying it backwards as he made his way to the shore; they watched the sun reflecting its rays off his golden coat that glistened with seawater and sprayed countless droplets as he shook time after time. The droplets rippled on the surface of a wave as it returned to its place of origin.

The group sat, taking in the rhythm of all that surrounded them. Later, as they lay back on the warm sand, Grace explained in words understood by the others the concept of matter. Betty, and Susie, no longer taken aback by what the child knew, listened with as much interest as did all the children. Grace gave a simple lesson in physics and something called neuro-psychoacoustics.

"All matter is made of atoms, atoms are molecules, and molecules are tiny bits of energy that are always moving — which means that matter has rhythm, a beat.

"And a beat makes a sound. Sometimes the rhythm it is so fast or slow that we can't hear or see it, but it is still moving and still making sound.

"That's why listening to things around you is important — even to things that you can't hear with your ears or see with your eyes.

"When someone is angry, their energy is different from when they're happy or sad. You can feel it if you listen quietly and you can help if you make your energy stronger than theirs.

"You can get them to match your calming rhythm, but it means you have to go into a deeper place in your heart, the place God made when He created each of us, the place where you keep your peace. We all have such a place, and once we know where it is, people can learn how to make it grow stronger so they can help others."

In the simplest of words, Grace had explained the concept of entrainment.

It was not long before the other adults in the family were anxious for a lesson from Grace. Sundays routinely became the day that all would gather at Henna and Albert's to listen to her words.

Soon her tender age did not matter for when she spoke there was no doubt that what she said came from another source and all knew that it came from God.

As the next few years passed, the family watched in great sadness the changes taking place in all aspects of society. A nearby shelter that had once served 75 people each night now had triple that number to attend to, as well as the need for additional facilities.

One day Grace, now barely nine, was helping Albert and Henna at the shelter when a fight broke out between two men who were arguing over the last bed available for the night.

"My kid needs a bed. You're nothing but a bum. I said it's mine."

The two began to fight, throwing punches but also hurling objects at each other. With the aid of another volunteer, Albert tried to pull them apart but without success.

One reached into his sock, pulled out a knife, and began to stab the other man several times before others in the crowd were able to pull the two apart.

The child of the wounded man screamed in horror as his father lay in front of him bleeding. Grace ran to the man and knelt down beside him. She surveyed his wounds quickly, and then laid her hands over each one; the bleeding stopped.

In silence and in awe the crowd stood watching what was happening before their eyes. When the man's wounds were closed, Grace continued to kneel at his side, whispering softly words that no one understood. When she was through, she looked up and glanced around the room at the astonished faces. The child of the man ran over and kneeled next to her.

"Thank you for helping my daddy."

And then it began: the cries from the crowd; the pushing to get to her; the pleading for relief from suffering caused by one thing or another; the people surrounded Grace, who had backed away from the man and child in fear.

Albert ran to her and gathered her up into his arms. He said not one word as he pushed his way to the door and out of the building to Henna who had raced to get the car. She opened the passenger side and Albert jumped in with a frightened Grace; the crowds swarmed around the car.

Albert yelled, *"Go, go on... they'll get out of the way, just go."*

Henna put her foot to the gas pedal and prayed out loud.

"God Almighty, make them move."

With that, Grace became herself. She sat up and looked through the car window at the faces of those who were pleading for help.

"Mama, wait, let me speak to them. I'm not afraid any more. I'll be alright."

Albert was not as sure as Grace was about how the crowd would receive her.

"Darlin', I realized a long time ago that you were different, but I don't think people are ready for the likes of you. Not yet."

Grace turned and took Albert's face into her hands; she looked at him and then at Henna and then spoke to them both.

"It's time for me to begin, whether we think I'm ready or not. I have so much to share with you but now I must help these people find hope tonight. I'll be alright, I promise you."

She smiled and added, "I have angels surrounding me wherever I go, and they won't let a hair on my head be touched."

Henna took her foot of the pedal and shut the car off. The crowd was taken aback, and even more so when Albert put the window down and asked those nearest the door to step back so he and Grace might get out of the car.

People stepped back and a man reached down and opened the door and offered a hand to Grace, who looked up, smiled and took it. She asked if they would return into the building so that all could hear what she had to say. Without a moment's hesitation, the crowd did as the child requested. She led the way back into the shelter with Henna and Albert on either side of her.

Inside, the injured man who had been made whole sat with his little boy on the coveted bed. He looked to Grace and nodded his thanks.

She went to him and held his head as he wept in her young arms. The crowd remained still; however, much whispering was heard throughout the room.

Grace lifted the man's face, wiped his tears, and patted the head of the little boy. She turned and began to speak.

"I know that all of you are suffering in one way or the other, and you want me to fix things, like you saw me do with him. But, I'm just a child and I don't know exactly what happened, exactly what took place, so it will be hard for me to explain things.

"All I know is that I saw a man in need and I went to him. I didn't think about what I should or shouldn't do, I just did.

"Inside of each of you is that desire to help one another, but, sadly, heaped on top of it is your own sadness and suffering. It gets in the way of the part of you that wants to give... To help someone else in need.

"There is energy in that part of your heart, the part that is loving and giving. This energy is like a force stronger than the mightiest wind. It takes time and practice to find that part of your heart, and patience... it takes a lot of patience."

Although stunned to hear such words from a child, they listened without interruption. Many had taken seats on the cots and floor of the room, sitting in a palpable silence. When Grace paused in her words, a hand went up from woman near the front and others followed likewise.

"But you're a child, how did you learn to do this at your age?

"Where are you from?"

"How come you ran away if you have such power?"

Grace began to answer the questions as simply and honestly as she could at this moment in time, knowing that too much information might cause even more question and more chaos.

"I was born here, right here in Bridgeport. I was adopted by Henna and Albert when I was a baby."

She looked at them lovingly.

"They've raised me and I've learned a lot from them."

The statement evoked another question from the crowd; this one was directed at Albert and Henna.

"Can you heal people too?"

Henna spoke with a great deal of thought.

"I'd like to think that I have healed many a wounded heart with my love and my touch. But to say I've done what Grace has done here tonight, no, I've not done that. In fact, if the truth were known, this is the first that Albert and I have seen such works. I'm startled by it myself, and I know and love the child."

She tried to lighten up the situation.

"You parents out there know kids today try to hide a great deal now, don't they?"

Then looking at Grace added, "Wait until we get home, missy, you have some explaining to do."

Many in the crowd genuinely laughed, breaking the tension. The people could see that Henna and Albert were no different from any of them, but the child, that was something else.

Grace smiled at Henna and then stood between her and Albert, waiting for them to take the lead. She knew that she had acted too quickly by healing the man but was at a loss at to how to explain to those who had witnessed it what had happened.

She whispered from her heart, "*Gyada, I need you.*"

That was all that was needed, and as promised by her spirit guide, help was there. Grace suddenly knew the words to say and stepped forward, as she let go of Albert and Henna's hands.

"What you saw was what God can do. It doesn't have to be in a big and beautiful cathedral or large auditorium with people raising up their arms in praise. It doesn't have to be ministers or priests or rabbi's, it can you, or you, or you."

She pointed to people in the crowd as she finished her last words, and then lastly pointed to the child of the man who had been stabbed, "Even you."

The little boy smiled at her but rather than hide got up and walked to her.

"Can you teach me to do what you did?"

Grace took a deep breath then said with confidence, "Yes, if you want more than anything in the world to become as God intended you to be, then yes I can teach you."

She looked around, pointed at each and every child in the room, and motioned them forward; there was at least two dozen from ages three to about 14.

"All of you will be easier to teach then any the older people, for you are closer to your beginning, closer to the intention of God for humanity. Not all of you will stay to learn, but I can promise you that if you want it, it will be so. And although what was you saw tonight was the healing of the outside of a man, what is more important is to heal the hearts of others, so that all can heal from within."

The children surrounded her and the adults stood back in silence.

It was enough. The evening came to an end for the three who had promised to return.

Everyone who spent the night at that shelter slept with a peaceful mind and a hopeful heart knowing that tomorrow would bring a brighter day.

Grace and Albert said little on the ride home, waiting for the comfort and security of their home before putting any questions to Grace.

In a way they weren't sure, if more questions needed asking but had a sense the child needed and wanted to speak.

And so, after she washed her face and put on her pajamas, Grace curled up on the couch in between her beloved Henna and Albert. She laid her head on his shoulder as she had done so many times, knowing that she had opened a door tonight that could not be closed.

She knew that she was putting them and the entire family into a situation whose outcome she could not predict. She took a big drink of air and let it out slowly then spoke. She addressed Albert first.

"Do you remember the morning you found me? You forgot most of what happened for a long time and since then you have seen things that were — well, that were hard to understand.

"I was sent here, to you, to your family for a purpose that I didn't fully understand, until tonight. I was sent here so that your family could teach me about how humanity was meant to live and to love among one another.

"You have taught me the love that is between a husband and wife, a mother and father, parent and child, brothers and sisters.

"I was sent here to learn from you and you have taught me so well. From the moment you held me your arms and let your tears fall on my face I felt your love and goodness."

Turning to Henna, Grace continued.

"It didn't matter that I did not come from you or even look like you, all you and the family saw was a child, a gift to be treasured, protected, and most importantly loved. You were right when you told the people tonight that you have healed many with your love and touch. You both have much to share and teach others at this time."

Henna closed her eyes before speaking, and then asked about Rachel.

"Is Rachel like you? Is she able to do the things you do?"

Grace thought carefully before answering, she used words that neither Henna nor Albert knew she had knowledge of.

"Rachel was chosen to teach people, especially women, in a way that will be easier for them to accept. Science is part of this world and there is a constant flow of new discoveries so her work will not be met with as much scrutiny. And sadly, given the position and attitude of men, they will dismiss much of Rachel's findings. However, her success will be apparent in the not too distant future."

Grace smiled and added, "She is quite remarkable, my birth mother."

Albert looked at Henna then at back at Grace. How could she know? It was never spoken of, never once was the story of Rachel and Grace mentioned.

He put his head down and tears began to run down his face. Given all that he knew of Grace, he felt that he might have failed somehow in keeping this information from her. Grace sensed as much and spoke gently to the man she knew as her father.

"I have always known. Even before Rachel came to live with us, I knew. We are connected in a way that goes beyond what is seen or heard."

Henna asked hesitantly, "Does she know that you know?"

"Yes, for several years, but it was not our place to tell you or the family of our knowledge... until now.

"All of her work at the University she has shared with me, and what I learn from Gyada, some is shared with her, but now a great deal will be shared with all of you."

Before either Henna or Albert asked, Grace shared with them who Gyada was.

"Gyada is my teacher. Her spirit speaks and guides me to become the Grace of God that will lead humanity through the times to come. The star that shone in the sky on the night of my birth brought great comfort to her, for it gave her knowledge of the coming of the awaited era of peace — a peace that would reign in the world she has watched over for a very long time."

"What will happen, here on Earth?"

Albert was unsure he wanted to know the answer to his question.

Grace spoke gently to the two people she loved so deeply.

"The physical changes that are taking place are part of a natural occurrence of the planet, of course because of the misuse and disregard for the incredible gifts resulting at creation, the changes have occurred earlier and much fiercer than designed.

"The waters, lands, and natural resources were meant to be equally valued as every life given. Sadly, though, that was not the case. The countless and ongoing advancements and discoveries through technology have been skewed by greed and misuse.

"There is no equal plane, thus creating unending inequities between those who have and those who have not. Each life is magnificent, each life precious beyond thought, yet humanity has removed the very essence that makes it so.

"It is the essence of God that has been smothered by the pigeonholes of inequity. You saw the faces tonight at the shelter. When the squabbling over a small cot brought about a savage attack on a fellow being, it was the result of a pervasive sense of hopelessness as well as hearts that have hardened by want of basic but material things.

"Yet, look how quickly they responded to what I did and yes, it was miraculous in their eyes, but when they began to listen to my simple words and to yours, it was the ache in their hearts and a deep unstoppable desire for the return of goodness and love to the world that allowed them to hear.

That incredibly powerful will, present in all, is what we will speak to, to reawaken their spiritual being, the God within. The spark may grow dim, but as I said to Rachel, the Goodness of God will never be extinguished."

The three sat in silence until Rachel walked through the door; it was nearly 11 o'clock. She knew immediately that something had occurred and nothing was said by anyone until Grace stood up, pulling with her both Henna and Albert. She was smiling as she addressed them all.

"Well, tonight begins a new part of our journey."

She threw her arms around both of them and then turned and looked at Rachel.

"We have much to do, but now we will have the whole family helping. I can't wait to see their faces when they hear we will all be moving west."

Henna and Albert both rolled their eyes in more wonderment before shooing Grace off to get ready for bed. After all, she was still only nine, and still in need of mothering and fathering even if she could do things that they never imagined seeing in their lifetime.

Grace did as she was told and when snuggled in bed she called out to them that she was ready for her "Good night."

Henna and Albert gave the usual hugs and kisses, but that night they all were aware that the life they knew had been changed forever.

It wasn't sadness or fear they felt —, no, it was more like a resolve to begin the last part of their own journey; and to do their part to help the others so the same.

A short time later, when Rachel peeked in on Grace, she found her sitting on the floor, facing the window, looking up at the moon.

Entranced, the child did not move. Rachel entered the room, closed the door quietly behind her, and lowered herself to the floor next to Grace. The child turned and smiled at her, took her hand into her own and spoke in a whisper.

"We have much to do. You must learn how to hear and speak to Gyada, she will guide you as she guides me."

"How do you know what you are hearing comes from her and not from your own mind?"

"I empty my mind so that Gyada only speaks to my heart, to my spirit. Our spirits receive only truths; there is no room for anything else."

"And where does *her* truth come from?"

"From Sophia, Wisdom, the source of truth... *I came out of the mouth of the most High and covered the Earth as a cloud. I dwelt in high places, and my throne is a cloudy pillar. I alone compassed the circuit of the sky and walked in the bottom of the deep; in the waves of the sea and in all the earth and in every people and nation... He created me from the beginning, before the world and I shall never fail.*"

Grace quoted from the Book of Ecclesiastics, as though the words were part of her.

"What if I cannot learn to be still? My mind is full of —"

"Much," Grace smiled and finishing her thoughts.

"I know, but now you will learn how to be still, allowing your spirit to guide you to become... To experience dharma, that which you are meant to be. You were created in such a way that it will be easier for you then most and tonight we will begin. Close your eyes, and see the moon without looking. See the dark sky that surrounds it, and the stars that glisten about it. Allow your mind's eye to hold the moon in its gaze, now breath slowly and deeply releasing all with each breath. Tonight we will be still."

All that is known you know

Knowing

*W*hen morning came the talk around the kitchen table was more somber than in days past until Grace brought a smile to everyone's face when she said, "The children are really going to love this new 'school' because there's not one book to read!"

This school was just one of many things that Grace told them about, and Henna had more than a few questions to ask. However, she thought it best to pace herself for fear of too much information.

Best deal with what she could see, hear and feel then do something practical to remedy it.

"I think we should call the family here tonight to let everyone know what happened at the shelter and to start getting ready for, well, for whatever we're getting ready for.

"In my heart, I can feel things are going to move really fast, especially when word gets around about last night. You can rest assure that they'll be twice as many people at that shelter tonight, and it won't be because they're looking for a bed.

"Albert, maybe you should look around for a building that's been abandoned for Grace and Rachel to use for their needs. And I think that maybe it's time we, the family, began looking at our living arrangements. We have a lot of space, rooms between us, it's time we opened our doors to others just as we're opening up our hearts."

Early that evening the family had the first of several meetings that would lead to plans that would alter their way of life, but not one among them — after hearing what took place at the shelter the night before — offered resistance.

They all knew that their Grace was special, now it was being made clear just how special she was. They also learned of Rachel's part, as best could be explained. Albert then spoke about the practical aspect of their new information and living arrangements.

The family — now 17 strong — maintained four households. By pooling resources since the recession began in 2001 all of the four houses that the family lived in were now paid for, much to the good planning of Albert and Betty.

They counted the number of rooms all told and decided that the 17 of them would be able to live in two of the houses and they would open the two remaining homes to others.

They decided to charge a minimal rent, but also determined not to turn away anyone who could not afford it.

The yards would become vegetable gardens everyone could tend for the benefit of all. Clothing that was not essential would be given away and shared; closet space would now be storage for canned goods that guests could use during the increasingly harsh and unpredictable winters.

Everyone had ideas to contribute and a willingness to pitch in wherever needed; Henna and Albert gave assignments out to all. The adults went about putting budgets and work schedules together.

Led by Grace, the young members of family drifted outside and gathered around the picnic table in the back yard. The youngest, eight-year-old Jeffrey, sat patiently waiting to hear how he was going to help others. He waited until there was a moment of silence then spoke hesitantly to Grace.

"You healed me, when we were little, didn't you?"

Grace smiled at him, overjoyed that he recalled the event.

"Yes. Why haven't you said anything until now Jeff?"

The others at the table were taken back by his remark. Every one of the youngsters — 11-year-old Jillian, 12-year-old Michael, the twins, Peter Jr. and Sam — who were now 13 — and Susie's oldest boy, Billy who turned 14 a few days before and Elizabeth, the eldest at 18 — listened intently to their young cousin's response.

"I thought I was dreaming it, or making it up. But after hearing what happened last night, I know it was for real. And if I close my eyes, I can see it just like it was happening right this minute. We were babies. In my crib, I stopped breathing and you helped me. Will you teach me to help others like that?"

Again Grace smiled, first at him, then looking around at the faces of the others.

"I'll try, but it will take work on your part. You have to put things away...things you think you know now."

Elizabeth, who was seated next to Grace, put her head down in thought, then lifted her head and looked into her eyes.

"Do you mean how we understand and see things now?"

Grace carefully chose her words as she spoke.

"Yes! Now, you only know what you see, and sometimes, you see, and then *think* you know, but then it turns out later that it's not really...the truth."

Michael added a question, "Does the same go for what we hear, touch and feel inside, like being happy or sad?"

"Yes."

Then she reminded him of the day at the beach.

"Remember when we sat very still and listened and watched to everything around us? You heard things that you never heard before allowing you to see things you had never seen before. That's the beginning part of learning to know, to listen with your heart and then the messages goes to a different place inside of you, not the place it goes to now."

Young Jeffrey pursed his lips and squinted as though trying to see what Grace was saying, then asked.

"Where does it go now?"

"It goes to kind of a file cabinet in your mind, where you collect all your — information. Every piece of information, things you see, hear, smell, touch, and even feel it all goes to the place inside of you that can understand the information. And you began collecting information before you were even born."

Then Grace's eyes lit up.

"Like the file cards you have for your dinosaur collection, Sam. You have a file box filled with cards and you keep them in categories from different eras.

"They're in alphabetical order and each card gives you information about each one. When you want to know about one you pull out that card. You know where you keep the file box and you know your alphabet so you know exactly where the information is. So it's easy. You do the same with information that you take in every moment of every day. Information you don't even realize is filed away, like if Grammy greets you at the door and smiles, what's going to happen next?"

The answer rushed out of Jillian. "She hugs you real tight and kisses both cheeks."

"How do you feel when she does that?"

Jeffrey jumped in. "Loved, happy."

Pete and Sam had a different view. "*Embarrassed.*"

But Billy added, "Yeah, but I still like it when she does it, and I don't even mind when Gramps does it. How come?"

Grace continued.

"Because the action is familiar and without even thinking you put it into your file cabinet and pull out a response," she gently tapped Billy's head and then his heart, "that holds the information that lets you react with the feeling and action that fits. You hug Grammy back, right?"

Pete Jr. wanted more, "How come, even if we feel embarrassed, we hug back?"

Elizabeth answered with a hint of a question in her voice.

"Because we all only know Grammy to be loving toward us, and that makes us feel really good and safe inside. Even you guys can't help but respond to that because that's what we've done from the beginning of knowing her.

"From the very first time she picked each of us up, we felt her love and we put that feeling inside so we don't even think about reacting any more, we just do. And it's why we act toward others the way we do, because that's what everyone else in the family has shown us, by their actions and words that just happen automatically...without thinking to be kind or loving.

"Like a few winters ago at school with Eddie Johnson. Sam, you were only 10 but you knew he didn't have a coat, and you gave him your own. You didn't think about being cold on the way home, you just did it and you *knew* your mom wouldn't be angry about it either."

Grace added the rest to help the younger ones to understand a bit more.

"Yes, that's it, you don't even think about things, you just do it, it happens that quickly. The same it true for tons and tons of other pieces of information or experiences that you've have had or your grandparents or your parents have had and passed onto you and the same is true for the ones you *will* have, new is really old. That's where everything you know is kept...*in the place, that just knows what is.* Just because you haven't seen, heard, or touched it yet, doesn't mean that you don't already know it. Your spirit holds all the information that you don't know what to do with — yet."

"You mean like what you did last night? Where does that information come from?" Billy asked.

Grace took a long, slow deep breath before she answered; she stood up then gathered some of small white gravel that lined the driveway and made a large circle in the grass. She took Jeffrey's hand and led him inside of it. One by one, she placed the others around him, some inside, some outside the circle and others she had stand a good distance away. Then, speaking clearly and with purpose, she began.

"If the circle Jeff is standing in is our universe," then she pointed to each one of them, "and you are the sun, and you the moon, and stars and other planets, how do you think it happens that nothing collides into each other and destroys everything for good?"

Michael ventured an answer. "Because when God made everything He planned... He laid it out, so it wouldn't do that."

Grace prodded him. "From the beginning, millions and millions of years ago God knew to do that?"

The boy continued unwavering.

"Yes, when He created everything, He planned it all to the very end. From the beginning to the end, He planned it all." Then he added what he learned in science.

"Planets and stars do collide but the Earth, for now, is okay."

"What about things like the — Ice Age?" Grace continued to push him.

"Well, when parts of the Earth froze, He planned how it would thaw out in the future which changed the mountains and oceans, but it's still here, right?"

Grace pushed again for her cousins to reach inside for what they knew to be truth.

"So, God would have had to know what was going to happen way into the future and plan for things to evolve, to change. Living things and the Earth were designed to adapt for times like when the Ice Age occurred or earthquakes, floods, or plagues. The same for wars that destroy almost as much; when the world around them changes people have to know how to change the way they live in that same environment in order to keep going... Keep living."

Grace was moving closer to her point. "When the world changes in ways that are not planned for, how come people still keep going and do not give up?"

"Because they adapt to the changes, they learn a different way to live." Sam answered as he and the others returned to the picnic table.

Grace went on. "Yes, but how do they know to do that?"

"Because that's what people know to do... to keep living; they have to eat, sleep, and wear clothes and other stuff so they figure out how to do it. It doesn't always happen right away, and sometimes other people have to help them and sometimes they have to learn a new way to live on their own, but that's why we're still here on earth, because we know how to keep living *here*."

Grace thought a moment before responding to Billy.

"Yes, we do, we really *know* how to live here. If from the beginning, human beings continued to go on living and adapting to changes, no matter what happens, where does the *knowing* to do that come from?"

Jillian piped up once again, absolutely sure of the answer. "From God, He made it so we could exist, live here forever no matter what, but I don't think we're supposed to live the way the world is now."

Silence took over when the reality of the state of the world entered the heart of each child. Grace continued.

"And what do you know about God?" Grace put the question to all of them and the responses came without much effort.

"That He is all good."

"... And all loving and is all things."

"He made us in His image, in His likeness."

Grace knew all of her cousins would understand the remainder of her words.

"Yes, Peter we are made just like God. And remember the file cabinet inside of each of you that collects information about things — silly as it sounds, if you can imagine God having a filing cabinet just like that — however, the big difference is God is the filing cabinet for all information!

"Before there was anything, and the moment there was everything ... All the information for all time was there, including us... we already were.

"Humanity is from the *knowing* of God, the Creator of all, so all that is *known* by God, is known by humanity. Other things experience the knowing as well but to the degree that they are part of the plan of All.

"That's why we know everything about existing here on earth as it was created. Just as trees know when to change the colors of their leaves and certain fish know to swim upstream to lay their eggs and birds, they know to fly south in the winter.

"Even the changes that happen to Earth, like fires, earthquakes, floods and big storms, even these have *knowing* about their purpose and part in the magnificent plan of ALL — what each must do to continue existing on this Earth."

"How come some people say that it's God punishing us when there are fires, or floods or wars; that he's angry for what we've done to one another and to the Earth?"

Michael paused then added these last few words to his own understanding of such.

"I kind of understand why He would be mad, though. People have gotten greedy and selfish and are mean to each other. And all the wars — I think we'll always be at war somewhere in the world, until we blow one another up. I wish that I could change that."

Grace went to him and put her hand on his shoulders before she spoke. "You can, Michael, and you will be part of that. That's why all of you are here, because your spirits know and desire humanity to evolve toward Oneness with the Creator. But first, we must know wholly what that is; not the idea of God that has been passed down for centuries or what has been written about him by others, but what it means to be the true Essence of God."

As Grace continued to speak, the others leaned in closely to hear her words.

"Throughout the ages great beings have been sent by the Creator of All to teach people, to show them what human beings can be and what they really are.

"Like Jesus!" Sam asked.

"Yes!" Grace responded with a smile and much joy. "He was the greatest of them. He was sent to Earth because humanity was growing in a direction far away from God. Jesus came to teach them about who they were and that they could become like him; but they crucified Him. But His message and His teachings took root and became the foundation of several religions. Years after His death men began to write down stories about Him in an attempt to share His teachings with others. Those words were written and then explained by those who thought they knew the truth behind His words. The greatest mistake made however was that they created a God that was out here or up there — far away from us.

"The major religions of the world have taught for centuries that God is separate — outside of humanity — and that no one can truly know or understand God. *But that is not true.* We know God, because humanity is an outward identical expression of what God is — which includes all Godly attributes and abilities. And God is not only Father, but is Mother and Son and Daughter—"

"Then why does everyone think he's only Father?" Jeffrey struggled to understand.

"Because men were in charge then and it made sense to create religions that were modeled after most civilizations, so sadly women and children were given little if any importance; they had no place in the Beginning of Creation nor in humanity's journey throughout time.

"It wasn't like this in all religions, but when Christianity was being shaped that was the path they chose. It didn't happen overnight, but finally at a significant time in history, a great Emperor wanted more land and more people in his kingdom, and he saw a good way to make that happen was though this new religion that was attracting followers.

"He instructed his religious advisors to write down the stories that had been passed down through the years. They had many, many stories, gospels to choose from but selected only certain ones that told the history of God and story of Jesus in the way they wanted it to be told.

She continued.

"These stories were to be the only authoritative words about God and Jesus. And to make sure that people read only these stories laws were passed and harsh punishments enforced on those that didn't do as such. The newly forming Christian church thought it would also be good to have a set of rules or ways to worship and honor God, the Father, written down for men to follow, so they could live better lives. But the image of this Father that was created made him seem demanding, punishing, and not very loving.

"Other groups had different thoughts about God but were not as strong or as large in number as those forming the Christian Church. They tried to offer a truer concept of what God is and how we should honor the roles of both men and women, but just like today, the more powerful of the two won. But we really didn't need to have rules written down and we didn't need to have men teach us how to honor God. The rules have done more harm than good in the moving forward of humanity toward knowing God.

"God is the Beginning, the first energy, the force that propels creation in full circle back to the Beginning; the force of God is love, energy in its purest form and is neither man nor a woman. God is all knowing, and we are part of all of that. And since we're part of that, humans know how to continue to live, how to adapt to the changes that have occurred throughout history, including those that are taking place now and those to come. All of that information is filed away inside of you just waiting to be used. That is where the information comes from, and you can't help but *know* it because you're part of it."

She finished with one last thing. "*Knowing is what we are.*"

When she was finished speaking not one of them looked afraid or perplexed, for the information they were given was drawn into the part of them that understood. Thus, the school began that evening; the founders were a few children, sitting in the early evening around a picnic bench and the only curriculum was learning to *know*.

~ ~ ~ ~ ~ ~ ~ ~ ~ ~

During the next few weeks, the family worked side by side in sorting through the four households to make the changes for their new living arrangements.

Al Jr. and his family moved in with Henna and Albert, leaving Ruthie and Susie and their families to share quarters. It was not nearly as difficult to let go of things as one would think for the family began to move as one, with the ultimate purpose of helping each other and anyone else that was in need.

The other two now-vacant houses had 16 additional rooms that Henna and Albert readied for others.

At one family meeting, the group discussed how they would select the new occupants. James was the first to offer comments.

"I think that we need to make sure that the people who live here will be expected to work and contribute to the pot that will be used for everyone. I could put something together that spells that out so there won't be any confusion or questions later on."

Ruth added her own thoughts to that, "But what if they have nothing coming in each month, and are not working? That is happening to so many people now, how do we turn away?"

"Everyone has something to give, even if it's not seen right off."

Henna relied on her wisdom to guide the others.

"Especially in need are the elderly, most are living with the bare minimum. Maybe we should divide up the rooms and make sure each we look at each type of family or person from all situations. I'm sure three elderly women wouldn't mind sharing one bedroom, or two single Moms. I think whoever finds their way to our door is suppose to be there. Do we really want more rules?"

"Your Mama's right, let's just put the word out there and see what happens," said Albert. "As Grace said, people were chosen to part of this moment in time and so I believe we will draw in those who will help and not hinder that what is suppose to be."

He looked to Grace and smiled tenderly, "Unless you think something differently, darlin'."

"Daddy is right," Grace replied. "When people feel wanted and loved, they tend to just give back more than they thought they could.

But, what will be important is trust. Everyone who becomes part of this family — and that's what we are doing, growing our family — will have to trust one another completely. There will come a time when that is essential and lives will depend on it."

Her last words, caused the others to sit a bit straighter, and breathe a bit more quickly. Betty asked for all of them a question she was not sure she wanted answered.

"Are there people who will try and stop us from helping others?"

Grace waited a moment before answering, seeing the looks on her family's faces.

"Yes, but not for any other reason than they are so far from the awareness of who they truly are."

She continued,

"This distance creates fear, that shows itself as anger that often becomes violent. This is why it is essential for all of us to develop a keen sense of reading the energy of those around us. A peaceful heart and spirit is present even in the direst of situation. The stronger you become within your being the more power you will have to avert a dangerous situation. And there will be many of those... I'm sorry Mama, too many people are too afraid. The power of a peaceful spirit infused with only radiant love and forgiveness is more forceful than any amount of fear. We will grow together to become warriors of peace, and we will lead others toward the same."

After Grace's comments the group decided to begin where the need was most obvious.

The next day, Albert and Al Jr. went to several of the shelters and hung up flyers the children had made that promoted the available housing.

Within several hours, hundreds of people were lined up outside, each waiting their turn to speak with Ruth and Peter at one and Susie and James at the other.

Applicants filled out a simple form that gave basic information about their own needs and what they might be able to contribute. And each prospective resident also learned that the latter would have no effect on the group's housing decision.

Henna and Albert stood in the living room of Susie's former home and looked at the faces of the people, all desperately wanting to be chosen.

"How do we turn so many away, Albert?"

"It doesn't seem right, but we're only one family Henna. We only have so much space to give. What worries me is how we're going to have to sift through so many to find a handful. Maybe we should leave it up to chance, put them all into a big box, and let the children pull out names."

"Now that's a very smart and fair way to handle this. I'll step outside and tell Susie and James and you run over and tell Ruthie and Peter. It will save a great deal of time and heartache no doubt."

A big cardboard box was soon filled with the names of those hoping to be lucky enough to become part of the family. Early that evening when the last form was dropped into the box, which was set at Ruth and Peter's front yard, the crowd mulled about waiting for the names to be called. The family gathered inside and Grace spoke.

"We are opening more than our homes tonight; we are opening our hearts to others who will become part of what we are to do."

She looked to Jeffrey, who was going to pull out the names. "Quiet yourself and allow your hand to seek the one who will join with us in harmony."

Then Albert spoke, as he took up the hands of those on either side of him, with the others following suit, "God, Almighty, within us and all around us, guide us to follow our *knowing* of what is planned to restore our world to peace. Help us to help others to know our truth."

The crowd became still when the family emerged. The 17 of them stood around the box, but before the first name was pulled, Henna stepped forward to speak.

"We know how badly all you want to hear your family's name called but the reality is that there are only 16 rooms in the two houses and two of those rooms are kitchens, and we all know we can't have people living where food gets cooked and eaten."

A few in the crowd laughed out loud, knowing this good woman was trying real hard to ease the pain of those who would who would return to the shelter or sleep outside if not called.

Henna went on, "I wish with all my heart that we had a space for all of you, but I want you to know that we will continue to reach out to all in any way shape or form that we can. So I guess all that's left is to begin. My grandson Jeffrey will pull out the names."

Jeffrey stepped forward, but before reaching into the box, he looked into the crowd and walked toward a little girl who stood in the front. He put out his hand and she took it.

"Will you help me do this?"

The child nodded and walked with him to the box. She raised her arm then closed her eyes then reached deep into the box pulling out the first form.

She handed it to Jeffrey. Their fingers touched; he looked at her and smiled then read it over. In a clear strong voice, he called out the first names.

"Willis and Mary Reagan, and their two children, Wills and Julia."

A cry went up in the crowd, "Thank you! Oh my God, thank you." A young family came forward and stood to the right of Henna who put her arm about woman.

Time and again the little girl reached in and waited as Jeffrey called out the name on the paper.

Jeffrey called the sixth name: "Helen Worthing."

An elderly woman stepped forward, carrying brown bags of her possessions. Before she took her place, she spoke, addressing the family.

"If it's alright, I don't mind sharing a room with a few others like myself — alone without family."

Henna moved to her side and embraced her warmly then spoke to the crowd.

"Are there any others like Helen who don't mind living with...well, strangers, but trust that notion will end soon?"

Another elderly woman stepped forward and a then another. Expressing much appreciation of the gift that they would know where they would lay their head each night. They stood on either side of Helen waiting to share stories of who they were and the lives they lived thus far.

There were still two rooms left to fill as the girl pulled out another form and stood quietly while Jeffrey called out the name. He could help but notice the tears starting to brim in her eyes as she handed him the piece of paper. Her lower lip quivered, knowing that her family had only one chance left to find a home.

Jeffrey turned and looked to Grace who smiled at him, and then gave a slight nod of her head, urging him on. When the little girl lifted her hand over the box, Jeffrey took it and held it fast in his own and with his other one he reached deep into the box, closing his eyes as he did so. He released a gentle sigh and slowly pulled out the last form from near the bottom of the box. He did not let go of the child's hand until he read out the name that was printed on the form.

"Rusty and Sharon Appleton and daughter Sarah."

Before he let go of her hand, he squeezed it gently so that she could run to her parents. A man in the crowd shouted out, "How did he do that?"

Another following suit added, "How could he know her name, it was fixed." Before another word was said, Jeffrey stepped forward to let his eight-year-old voice be heard.

"No, I didn't know her name, I never saw her before tonight, but if you listen I'll try to explain what happened."

His gentle approach quieted the crowd who was now eager to hear what the boy had to say.

"When I first stood in front of Sarah I reached out my hand to her and she took it. She didn't think about it, she just reached out to me. Each time she handed me one of the forms our hands touched. I could feel inside of me what she was feeling. I felt her joy for each one of those whose name I called. Her joy was real, it was unselfish, and even during the last moments when there was one space last her thoughts were not for herself but for her mother and father."

Before Jeffrey went on, he looked at Sarah, seeking a silent permission to reveal something personal about her family; she lowered her head before nodding yes.

"You see, Sarah's father is ill, and all she wants is for him to have a bed, the same bed each night where there are people around him. I felt her incredible love for him and that love poured out of her into me so that I could seek out their form among the hundreds in the box."

"How could you just reach in and pull his out?" Someone asked from the crowd.

Before he could answer, Grace stepped forward and stood by his side, she spoke the words to help all to understand and to calm them.

"Jeffrey reached in while holding on to Sarah's hand, took on her energy then sought out the same in the box."

Grace took the paper from Jeffrey's hands and without even looking at it, knew that it was Sarah who had filled out the form. She held in front of the people so they could see for themselves the writing of an eight-year-old.

Then she asked Sarah, "Why didn't your Mom or Dad fill it out?"
Sarah looking a bit frightened answered quietly,

"They didn't think that you would want someone who was sick, but I told them it wouldn't matter to people like you. If people are willing to open their homes to others then they must have really big hearts and hearts like that don't turn away anyone. So I made them come here and told them I would take care of things."

She looked around and smiled from ear to ear before adding, "I guess I did a good job, huh, Daddy?"

Rusty Appleton could not speak because the tears that streamed down his face had caused his heart to swell so full that words would not come. Albert spoke for the man.

"You did a really fine job, Miss Sarah, and not to worry, for your Daddy and Mama are going to have a place for as long as they need. And soon your heart will be able to do what Jeffrey did tonight, for when the time comes it will be you reaching out to another in need."

The crowd was satisfied. No more words were necessary and soon the only people left were the chosen ones. Helen, the elderly woman spoke up first.

"Well, here we are, now what do we do? Just put us where you think we'll work out the best for all. I think I can speak for all of us, in that this gift you have given each of us can not be measured or weighed so to say thank seems inadequate. However, you can rest assure that it be evident in the manner in which we begin sharing the ups and downs of learning to live with one another. But my age and upbringing is ringing loud and clear and so I am compelled to say a loud and resounding thank you. Thank you from the bottom of my heart."

The new people surrounded the family and the joy and love expressed could have lit the night sky. Laughter rang through the neighborhood as the family divvied up house and room assignments.

In the next few days, the family and residents moved beds and dressers from one house to the other, from one room to the other until all were settled in.

Next came division of chores, responsibilities, and contributions no matter how small was pooled into one pot to handle the monthly expenses. Anything left would be used for the benefit of all. The family helped where and when needed and kept each house informed of all news.

Residents turned an abandoned restaurant into a meeting place that could hold the entire group, which now numbered 41 people, with one on the way. They gathered each night to make sure everything was being taken care of, without anyone or thing being overlooked.

For the most part things went smoothly until one meeting Albert shared an encounter he had with a city official who was making a great deal of noise about so many unrelated people living under each roof.

"I didn't say anything at first, which I think made him even madder, then, I looked him in the eyes and said, each and everyone of these folks, is my kin. And I began rattling off each of your names and telling him how we were related, and whose uncle was married to whose cousin, and whose great-great grandmother was aunt to my mother.

"I went on and on, and the poor man didn't know which way was up. Thankfully, Grace came and Rachel just happened to come home and it sure helped when my sweet little child ran up and said, 'Hi, Daddy!'

"I tell you, the man's head is still spinning. So, I'm telling you this just in case someone, him for example comes knocking at the door causing nerves to tremble. We're all related in one way or another and that's that. You can refer to me as Brother Albert, or cousin Al.

"How you wish to create your particular family tree does not matter, if fact the more elaborate the better. I don't think he was really trying to cause trouble; he was just doing his job. Wait until we start growing our gardens — my oh my!"

Laughter spread around the room as several new members introduced themselves to the group. The children had the most fun; however, it was Grace who stood quietly observing the newly created family with a deep knowing that things had just begun.

While the adults met in one room of the restaurant, the children would gather in another where Grace would talk to them. She explained the same things to the new children in the same manner she had with her cousins.

After witnessing the event at the drawing there was a more open reception to all things she had to say. Later in their respective rooms or houses, they would share with the adults all that Grace had said to them. Their simplicity and sincerity diminished all doubt, for there was a palpable peace in all dwellings when the children spoke.

One evening, after all gardens had been watered and the last dish dried, the children gathered in the parking lot of the restaurant for a game of tag.

They played for a while when suddenly a group of four others showed up. The newcomers stood and watched as the others played until Sam, called out to them.

"Come on, you want to play? The oldest one, a boy who looked to be around 14 stood back while the younger ones after getting a nod of approval from him quickly joined in the game. Sam approached the boy with an extended hand.

"Hi, my name is Sam. Do you live around here?"

The boy gave Sam a weak handshake, then pulled it back quickly, and shoved both hands into the pockets of a much worn pair of shorts. He lowered his head and mumbled his name and answer to Sam's question.

"Jake. Not really."

Sam kept going, "We all live a couple of blocks from here. We're… We're all, uh — cousins."

He quickly remembered his grandfather's cautionary words of explaining this newly-formed family. He also observed that the boy looked weary beyond his years and no doubt in need of a good meal, as were the others. "Are they your sisters and brother?"

"Yes. I take care of them when our folks are away. They'll be back tomorrow, they went to visit my grandmother in New York."

Sam had seen the look too many times in the shelter to know that this young boy was on his own and trying to care for his siblings the best he knew how.

He knew he needed help but did not want to scare the boy off. If Henna was here, all it would take would be one look and she would know exactly what to say. He had to find the words inside, words he already knew to say.

"I was wondering if you have a minute to give me a hand back at my house with something. I am trying to figure how to best use this great piece of plywood I found in my grandfather's garage. We need to get rid of it for space but it seems a shame to just to throw it out. My cousins can't decide what to do with it so maybe a fresh set of eyes laid on it will figure it out. I mean if it's not asking too much. Do you have the time?"

"I can't leave them alone," He said, motioning to his brother and sisters.

"Well, they can come along, that will be just fine."

He went over to Pete, Jr. and Michael and then to Grace, informing them that he was heading back to the house. The game stopped and all the children, as though in a parade, marched back to Henna and Albert's house.

The garage was nearly empty, but as Sam relayed there was not one but several pieces of good sturdy plywood. Jake looked at it closely and heaved a big sigh then bravely spoke.

"You could make a good floor out of this, and a bed off the ground. It wouldn't take much and this piece of two by four could be cut into legs. If you want, I could get rid of it for you. It will take a couple of trips but I could haul it off for you."

"A bed! Now why didn't you think of that, Pete? That's a great idea especially since we're going to turn this garage into more living space for people to use. Gramps will love the idea. Hey, Jake, maybe you could stay for awhile and talk to him. I bet he would let us use his tools. Can you stay? If you live to far to walk home later, I'm sure he'll give you all a lift."

Jake's littlest sister spoke up in a voice that was filled with tears.

"We don't have a home anymore. They threw us out last week when Mommy and Daddy didn't come back."

Jake rushed to his sister and put his arms around her.

"Shhh, you don't know what you're saying. They're coming back. Tomorrow, they'll be back tomorrow, Katie."

Sam moved next to Jake and put his hand on the boy's shoulder. "You can stay here with us. We'll make room for you in the house until we fix up out here. My grandparents won't mind, they won't mind at all.

And so this is how the family grew. People were drawn to the circle of compassion and goodness that flowed from house of Henna and Albert.

By the end of summer, six other families in the neighborhood opened their homes to others and all worked together to pay the bills, share the workload, tend the gardens and listened to the words of Grace and observed the children, who without coaxing or cajoling became the solid foundation on which all stood.

It was not complicated, there were no committees, nor votes nor letters of discontentment, for it was more than evident that all else had failed and there was no room for anything but compassion and love. The number of adults was had grown to 82 and the number of children stood at 64.

However, things were about to change.

~ ~ ~ ~ ~ ~ ~ ~ ~ ~

One morning in the third week of October 2008 began as any other day for people in homes across a country that had grown accustomed to the unexpected, grown accustomed to sorrow and strife. But most could not wrap their minds around what occurred in one of the greatest cities in the world before noon on that Wednesday.

Albert left for work at his usual time; Henna, Grace and the others now living in the house slept until the morning light woke them. Grace tiptoed into Henna's room, crawled under the covers, and snuggled up close to her.

"Morning, sweet child," Henna pulled her close and whispered into her hair, "and what shall we do today?"

"Well, first we need to stay right here and be still. Listen Mama, to the sound of the morning isn't it beautiful. I wish everyone would be still so that the sound of morning could be heard around the world."

"Baby girl, if anyone can make the sound be heard it will be you. So, what say we set our feet onto the floor and begin breakfast, I can hear Jeffrey from here making his mark on the coffee cake I made yesterday. If we dawdle in bed there won't be a crumb left."

Inspired by the taste of Henna's cake pushed Grace to throw back the covers and leave only wisps of footprints on the floor as she raced into the kitchen.

"Hey, leave something for us."

"I am. I'm leaving the design on the plate."

Jeffrey came back with one of his grandfather's retorts, which caused a giggle from Grace.

"Well, I'll be sure to tell Grandpa that when he lifts the tin cover and finds nothing to eat but a bunch of pink flowers." Henna entered the room.

"Mama, Jeffrey is sounded just like Daddy and goodness knows one of him in the house is enough. Right?"

"Sweet Jesus, child, one of Albert on this side of the world is more than enough for entire planet. Now, are you two coming with me to the center? I'm planning on leaving exactly at 9; not 9:15 or even 9:05, but 9 on the nose so be ready or I leave you to the master of assigning chores — Ruth."

"Oh Grams, no, you can't do that, my mama is always making me do things. *Lift this, pull that, Jeffrey, come here and bring the boxes down to the basement, no they don't fit right in the basement, bring them up to the attic.*"

As the boy mimicked the sound of his mother's voice, Henna and Grace filled the kitchen with their laughter. Ruth pushed opened the swinging door with her hands on her hips.

"Okay, I can only imagine my son is poking fun at his own Mama that would cause such a ruckus. Is that what you're doing mister?"

"Oh, no Mama, I would never do anything like that. Would I, Grandma? Hey, Mama you want the last piece of coffee cake, it's really good. Grace was trying to take the last piece but I said, no way you have to save a piece for my sweet Mama."

Henna threw her arms around the boy and pulled him in close. "You know Jeffrey the penalty for lying around here is kitchen duty for two weeks straight. Ain't that right, Grace?"

"That's right and you know who you have to do it with? Grandpa!"

On that last word, Al, Jr. and Elizabeth joined the trio in the kitchen. Elizabeth spoke first.

"Poor Grandpa, he gets blamed for everything, even when he's not here. Mama, are you coming into New York with us this morning? Rachel is taking the train from New Haven and we're going to get on when it stops in Bridgeport. I can't wait to check out the University. She says it has one of the best libraries for research. Grace, do you want to come along?"

"Can I, Mama? I love the train. And we'll be back from the Center by Noon, right? Unless you need me here, I'll stay if you need me."

"You can certainly ride the train with the others. I'll even take you to the station after the Center. That leaves Jeffrey and me to handle the rest of the work this afternoon."

Still wrapped in her arms, the little boy let out a groan, but still managed to hook his arms behind his grandmother's, lean backward and lift head to give her a big smile.

Al, Jr. reminded Elizabeth of their schedule. "I don't know if you're going to have time to go the Center Grace, we were planning on taking the 10:20 train in to Grand Central."

Grace threw her arms around Henna and Jeffrey had no choice to but to be included in the embrace.

"Mama, can I go tomorrow to the Center, please —"

"Oh, for goodness sake child, when have I ever said 'No?' 'Course, I wouldn't mind going myself but it gonna have to be next time. I've made too many promises to folks at the shelter for things happening there today. That's okay, I've got my nice strong Jeffrey to help lift the bags and boxes into the car."

Another groan emerged from the boy now locked in the middle of big a hug.

Grace planted a kiss soundly on his cheek. "Oh, sorry Jeffrey, that was supposed to be for Mama."

She pulled away and ran out of the room with Jeff racing after her.

"Will you all be home for dinner?"

"I would imagine we'd be back by early evening, unless the ladies make an unscheduled detour. Being the only male tagging along I don't think I'll have much say, will I now."

The time passed quickly and before long, Ruth took the trio to station.

"Keep your cell phone on, so I can check in with you all, to know everyone's still alive and well."

She kissed them goodbye and headed off. The train arrived from New Haven 15 minutes later and as planned, they joined Rachel on the second car from the rear. Her face lit up when Grace waved to her from the door of the train. The time was 10:20 AM the train was due to arrive at Grand Central at 11:31.

"Hi, sweetie, I'm so glad you came along. I don't get to spend enough daylight hours with you with all the time at the laboratory. Wait until you see the library at this school, it's over five stories high, and you can look up at all of them just standing in the middle of the foyer."

Once they pulled out of Stamford, the train ran express, stopping at 125th Street then on to Grand Central. Grace took a seat next to Rachel and Al, Jr. and Elizabeth sat across from them. There were 15 other people in the car, some reading, a few sleeping but nothing out of the ordinary going on. One half hour passed, the time was 10:49.

Grace began to look around, first, to the front then to the back of the car. Sensing something was troubling her Rachel put her arm around her shoulders.

"Are you okay?"

Grace smiled nervously up at her, and then whispered softly, "Will you take me to the bathroom, please?"

She took Rachel's hand, the two walked toward the front of car, and then on through the door to the next one; when the door closed behind them, Grace stopped them.

"Something is wrong, Rachel. Something is terribly wrong. Can you feel it?"

"I can only sense that something is upsetting you. What is it that you feel? Is someone sick on the train?"

"No, it's not in here, it ahead of us. We can't go there; we cannot let the train go into the station. We have to stop it, now, Rachel. We have to stop the train!"

Rachel was kneeling in front of Grace, looking into her eyes, and seeing a great amount of fear.

"How? What can we do to stop the train?"

"I don't think they'll believe me if I just tell them I know something is going to happen, but maybe they'll believe you. We have to do something to stop the train. It will be too late if we wait until we get to the next stop."

She began to cry in a way Rachel had never seen before. Not sobs or great heaving moans, but still her tears flowed.

"So many people – will die... Be hurt... I can't help them, Rachel, I can't help them all."

Rachel gathered her into her arms and held tightly to the child who carried the suffering of many her small body. She scooped her up and then sat down in the closest seat and spoke loudly to the others in the train.

"I need someone to get an attendant. I have a very sick little girl. I need to get her to a hospital. Please hurry. Get some help. We need to stop the train."

A man raced out of the car and was back with an employee of Metro North.

"What's the matter with the child?"

"She's having a severe reaction to a medication that I gave her this morning. I'm a doctor, but I don't have the necessary drugs to counteract the medicine. You've got to stop the train now! Please — I need to get her to a hospital."

"We'll be coming up to a hospital in New York in just a bit; will she be okay until then?"

Rachel, although very much in control raised her voice so others might join in her plea to stop the train. "No! You have to at least stop it here and let me get her off so I can get an ambulance for her. She is going to die if I don't treat her with the proper drugs."

A woman, now leaning over the seat behind Rachel spoke up loudly.

"Stop the damn train. Can't you see this child is ill? Stop the train or I will pull the switch myself."

The man spoke into his walkie-talkie an urgent code. "Code Red in Car 7 — I repeat Code Red in Car 7. Stop the train. I repeat stop the train now. Everyone brace for stopping. Brace for stopping."

The 10 cars of the 10:20 train out of Bridgeport came to a screeching halt. It was now 11:19; the train was approximately 17 miles from Grand Central Terminal.

"Please get my family, my niece and her father in the second to last car, they're in the last seat of the car. Tell them Grace is ill."

The woman whose insistence had stopped the train ran back to get Elizabeth and Al, Jr. The two were at Rachel's side in moments.

"What wrong, what's happened to Grace? Let me take her, she must be heavy for you." Al lifted the limp child into his arms and cradled her gently. He looked at her face, which was now pale and cool, he knew immediately that something was very wrong and not so much with Grace but around her.

"The Engineer called an ambulance and it's on its way, Doctor. Is there anything we can get for you?"

"No, thank you, I think just a little air will help, perhaps you could open the door of the train for ventilation. And if you don't mind, the other people in the car, perhaps they might move to the next one. And thank you for your help."

The car was cleared immediately, giving the family a moment to speak freely. Although Grace was indeed weak, she quickly repeated to the others the extreme danger that lay ahead of the train.

"We can't let the train go forward. We have to delay it a few minutes longer, and then it will stay here on its own. It won't be able to go forward to Grand Central."

The sound of a siren was getting closer; the time was 11:25. The train moved slowly backward toward a more level landing so that the EMT could board the train more easily with their gear. They entered at the first car and made their way back to where Grace and the family waited. By the time, they were at the child's side it was 11:28. Rachel stood to speak to them.

"I need to stabilize her before we transport, do you have saline so I can start an IV?"

"We thought we would carry her to the ambulance and work on her there so the train can get going."

"No, she needs fluid now, please go get it."

The EMT looked at his partner and gave a resigned look; they knew better to question an MD.

More importantly, they would not take the risk of injuring a child. The young female EMT took off for the requested supplies. She raced through the cars of the train and jumped off continuing her sprint to the ambulance, she pulled open the door, climbed in and grabbed what she needed.

As she turned to leave, she felt a rumbling beneath the truck. As she steadied herself, the blare of emergency sirens began from the town nearby.

The dispatcher screamed into the radio, his voice at a frenzied pitch, "Oh, my god, oh my god, all available crew, come in, come in. Anyone hearing this - come in, Code Zero, New York City; I repeat Code Zero, New York City. Come in, come in."

The young woman raced to the front of the ambulance and grabbed the receiver, "This is Weaver on unit 44, what's going down? What's happening in New York?"

"Terrorists have hit the city with bombs, Grand Central, bridges, downtown, the subway...can you leave the scene?"

"We had to board a train that was heading into Grand Central, they had a 10-year-old with some kind of a drug reaction, she needs to get to hospital, there's a family member with her who's an MD. I'll give her what she needs and get a local resident to transport her. Where do we go from here?"

"Head into the city, I'll get the route for you by the time you back into the rig. Go."

The girl ran back with everything she thought Rachel would need and prayed that the kid would be okay. Her mind was on New York and what she would find when they got there. She remembered the images from September 11, 2001 and shuddered at the thoughts of it happening again. The engineer met her at the door of the train.

"Did you feel it? What was it?"

"*New York, they hit New York again. Grand Central, a couple of bridges, subways, more buildings but...* "

"Oh, my God, we would be just pulling in...Oh my God, This stop saved us — saved us all."

The two made their way back to the Grace, who was now sitting up on Al's lap. Rachel was taking a wet cloth and wiping her face.

"Look's like she making a recovery. What happened?"

Grace looked into the eyes of the Engineer and spoke softly. "I had to stop the train, sir; I didn't know how to explain it to you. I couldn't let you pull into Grand Central."

One of the several people that had gathered in the car spoke up for the others.

"What is she talking about, what's happened in the city? What was that rumbling we felt?"

The young EMT began to cry as she spoke.

"Terrorists have hit New York again, this time with bombs all over the city. They blew up Grand Central, subways, bridges..." She could not go on.

The gasps and screaming began. The Engineer bent down and spoke softly to Grace. "How did you know?"

"I could feel the energy of the people who were going to die or be hurt. I could see the bombs exploding all over the city."

Now Grace began to wipe the tears with the back of her hand. Then she wiped the tears from the face of the Engineer.

"Thank you, thank you for..." His voice became inaudible.

Rachel put her hand on his shoulder. "Do you think you should tell the others on the train? Perhaps they have families that think they are in the middle of it all." She looked at Al as he dialed his cell phone. He shook his head, no signal. "They must have hit the towers. We've got to get word to the family that we're okay."

At the moment of the attack, Albert was in the middle of making a scheduled security check. Sirens began to blare urging him to race back to the security center. The news of the attack on New York filled the command center television monitors and two-way radios. The plant went into lock down; the reality of being a target of a terrorist attack was taken very seriously after 2001. He did not know of the train ride into New York City.

Henna, Ruth and Jeffrey were heading back to the house when the sirens began. They tuned in the radio as the announcer's broken voice gave the news.

"New York City has been hit again by terrorists. Just moments ago, a series of explosions, believed to be bombs planted throughout the city, leveled subways, bridges, hotels, theaters. Grand Central Station is completely demolished.

"The Department of Homeland Security, federal, state and municipal emergency management authorities are urging people to stay where they are. All access roads in and out are shut down and considered unsafe.

"I repeat: do not attempt to enter New York City from any direction. And people of New York if you are in my range, do not, I repeat do not attempt to leave the city.

"All roads, bridges, and any form of transportation is considered dangerous. Motorists, if you are on a bridge, please turn off your car engine and walk to the closest side of the entrance or exit.

"Turn off your engine and walk — don't run, don't panic, please — just walk to the closest side of entrance or exit.

"My God, what have they done to us? I repeat, New York City has just been hit by a series of explosions – presumably bombs — placed throughout the city, which exploded simultaneously at 11:31 this morning. There are numerous casualties, too many to guess at this early hour, and many unconfirmed reports of other explosive devices all over Manhattan. Wherever you may be, please remain there and keep monitoring your radio or TV for further information."

Henna pulled into the driveway and turned off the car. No one moved. No one spoke. Ruth reached into her purse pulled out her cell phone to see if it was turned on; it was. There were no messages. She pushed several numbers, then stopped before completing the call. She lowered her head and began to cry. Henna reached for her.

"Shhh. They'll be okay. Remember, Grace is with them. Our sweet Grace. Give me the phone."

She took the phone and dialed Al Jr's number; it rang a funny ring three times then stopped. She tried again. And again.

"Maybe the towers are down, Gram."

Jeffrey spoke quietly from the back seat.

"I bet there's no service, Mom. That's why we can't get through to Dad."

He reached forward, put his arms around his mother's neck, and buried his face into her hair. "He'll be okay, Mom. Grace will take of them all."

The Engineer gave the news over the loud speaker and as the EMT began to leave, Rachel stopped them.

"Are you heading into the city?"

"We were, but I just got word that all road are closed even to emergency vehicles, they all have to be checked for more bombs."

She softened her voice to almost a whisper then added, "They also told you some of the explosives contained biochemical weapons that are already airborne."

Rachel looked at the two young emergency technicians, both appeared anxious to help but unable to do anything.

"Perhaps we should go through the train and see if anyone needs help. I can only imagine this news has got to been devastating for everyone… Maybe we could help that way."

Grace looked at Rachel and motioned with her eyes for her to come close.

"I can help, let me come with you."

Rachel took her hand and the two followed the EMTs who didn't even question it. They looked at Grace and nodded, truth be known they felt safer that the child was with them, or that they were with her. The group made their way through the cars checking on all. The grief and outrage was palpable. When they reached the first car, the engineer was on the radio talking to his dispatcher.

"Alright, yes, until further notice we stay where we are."

Rachel noticed ahead of them was another train on Northbound side of the tracks. It too was stopped.

"Is that one returning to Connecticut?"

"Right now, none of the trains are going to move. They want to make sure there are no bombs planted anywhere. That one left Grand Central five minutes before it exploded. They've got bomb dogs coming in to check it out." He looked at Grace.

"Can you tell… If something is going to happen on that one?"

"It's safe. They're all safe over there. But I was wondering, do you think you could get me into the city somehow? I could help people. I could try to help all those in the tunnels who are still alive. I could show the others where they are, could you help me do that?"

The Engineer didn't even hesitate a moment. He picked up his microphone and called Metro North Head Quarters.

"Put me through to the Commander. This is Priority One. I repeat this is Priority One."

In less than ten seconds, a voice came over the speaker.

"This is Commander Ellis, who am I speaking to?"

"Engineer Robert Stippe, on the 9:50 out of New Haven."

There was silence on the other end.

"Yes, that's right, the 9:50 — due in Grand Central at 11:35."

"My God, how… what happened? We thought you were gone with the others."

"That's why I'm calling, sir. I've got the reason we're all safe on this train standing right next to me. A child, a little girl named Grace. Somehow, someway this girl saw what was going to happen and got us to stop the train. She said she could see what was going to happen, she could feel the energy of the people dying, and hurting. She says she can help in New York if we can get her there."

"What do you mean? What can she do? Is she there? Let me speak to her. Grace, can you hear me okay?"

"Yes sir. I need you to help me get to New York… To the tunnel that leads into Grand Central. There are lots of people down there and they're alive — for now."

"Well, Grace, I appreciate you wanting to help but we're not sure if there are more bombs or not, I couldn't put a little girl in danger."

"You don't understand, I can tell if there are bombs, I can feel and hear them miles away, that's how I knew what was going to happen, the closer we got the clearer they became to me. I can make it safe for others to look and help the people trapped down there. You have to let me help — please, sir."

Her voice began to crack and tears began to fall down her cheeks. Rachel took the receiver from Grace.

"Sir, my name is Rachel, I am Grace's aunt, and I am also a doctor. This child is special; she has abilities unlike anyone you could ever imagine. I would not put her in harm's way for anything and so with complete confidence I tell you, no I beg you, please allow her to do this. I will be at her side and take full responsibility for whatever happens. She saved the lives of the people on your train. Allow her to save others trapped in your tunnels."

The man on the other end was silent for only a moment. "Stippe, I'll send a chopper to your location, expect it in seven minutes from Westchester. Have them on the top of the first car and someone there to help them into the gear. Grace, God bless you child, God bless you."

"Wait, don't hang up. Will you call my family, tell them we're safe."

"Of course child, give Engineer Stippe the information, and I personally will make the call."

The communication ended and shortly thereafter, the sounds of a helicopter were heard overhead.

Grace and Rachel did what they could do that day, and for weeks later but the reality could not be changed.

Terrorist had hit New York again. This time it manifested as simultaneous biochemical and dirty bomb attacks which erupted throughout the city. The initial death toll was 27,852, but grew steadily, with an exact count impossible due to the prolonged effect of the biochemical weapons used; the city was placed under thirty days of quarantine. The grief and horror felt throughout the world from this assault on humanity would never lift from the spirit of the earth.

*T*he timing of the beginning of the new school was not a coincidence, the plight of the children in the country and through out the world who were at risk or in danger reached a staggering number.

In the United States at the start of 2010, there were over three million children in a National Foster Care System. State run programs no longer had the funds or ability to manage the number of cases reported or dumped in their laps. They became ineffective when more children were dying or being abused while under their auspices.

Child pornography continued to be one of the world's largest-grossing and fasting-growing businesses. The 2002 U.S. Supreme Court ruling upholding the rights for Internet companies who provided virtual reality child pornography sadly paved the path for such.

Child sex slaves and child brothels could be easily found in every major (and minor) city in the world. Affluent white businessmen who previously ventured into foreign countries for sex with children could now obtain it right in their own backyard. Crimes committed by adults against children continued to rise, however, violent acts by children became rampant.

Schools approached the drastic increase in violence in several ways. One was to shorten the day to four hours to lessen the liability of the Board of Education, while in the wealthier areas they lengthened their days to nine hours, allowing for a one half-hour pick-up before and after school for working parents.

Most had extensive security systems including police on campus, cameras, metal detectors, drug dogs, random raids, and urine tests. In the fall of 2009 a national mandate from the Secretary of Education and Director of Home Security, which was signed by the President, banned the use of all lockers, in all schools in America; the direct result of an event that occurred in the previous spring in Cleveland, Ohio.

In May of that year, several students at a junior high successfully executed an all out attack at their school. With the use of bombs, biochemical weapons and machine guns, seven middle school children succeeded in killing 433 students and 151 members of the faculty, leaving an additional 491 children and staff injured to varying degrees of severity. The perpetrators, three 13, two 14, and two 15-year-old students all survived.

They were tried, found guilty and condemned to death shortly there after. All seven were executed by lethal ejection in May of 2008, on the one-year anniversary of the massacre. The governor of Ohio did not have one person or any groups speak out against the death penalty on the children's behalf, nor would she have listened if that had been the case. It no longer mattered in the country that children were executed or tried as adults.

The death penalty had been reinstated in all but three states by the year 2008, mostly due to the 195 percent increase in murders and violent crimes across the nation in a period of only three years. In addition, the prisons in the country could no longer contain the number of persons incarcerated each year. The increase of criminal activity was no doubt directly related to the staggering 13 percent rate of unemployment. The numbers increased daily.

The country now had a population of old and young in need of help for the bare basics. The largest population, those over 65, was hit hard; earned pensions with health insurance vanished. The Department of Social Security announced that as of January 2010 funds would no longer be available; Medicare and Medicaid funds vanished as well.

The military drew more and more enlistments. The war in Iraq did not end in the summer of 2004, as was predicted by the Administration, but continued to rage on with casualties now in the thousands. The borders of the war had spread far beyond their expectations and there was no end in sight and the stockpiles of weapons of mass destruction?

They were eventually found, but not in the country of Iraq; Hussein's allies horded the nuclear warheads and biochemical weapons for him and began to use them in the spring of 2008.

In addition, the other threat back in the early 2000's, North Korea, made good on its word and forced the American troops out of the demilitarized zone in a disastrous battle that occurred in June of 2009 resulting in 4,876 of our soldiers dying in combat.

The United States and its allies continued to suffer attacks by terrorists who now held much of the world hostage. Racial profiling escalated to a pathetic frenzy throughout the world. If one did have the funds to travel, the security checks began from the moment a trip was planned or a ticket purchased. Everyone was suspect and everyone suspected the worst of his or her neighbor, be it the house next door or the country across the ocean.

It was not only the fact that much of humanity was struggling against manmade disaster but things out of their control greatly added to feelings of hopelessness.

Natural disasters were so commonplace that the Red Cross and other disaster relief organizations ran out of money when earthquakes, both on land and water hit simultaneously in five regions of the world in 2009. The tsunami of December 2004 began the natural rollercoaster ride that has yet to end.

By 2012, the state of California was reduced in size by two-thirds. Fire, floods, mudslides, and earthquakes began to swallow up land, which began in the nineties and grew in frequency and intensity over the past decade. No longer the state of sunshine and oranges it now was known only as Death Valley.

On the East Coast, Florida, once the premiere state for retirees from around the country was now a series of ghost towns along the shores. The hurricanes of 2004 began a downward spiral from which many businesses and residents could not recover.

The rest of the country suffered on going flooding and record-breaking periods of artic cold with snow falls measured now in feet not inches. Droughts caused water shortages leaving lawns brown and lakes dry. Hundreds of thousands of acres of forest burned yearly, destroying homes and businesses in the path of fire.

Gasoline was a luxury and people who were lucky enough to work, had to cut back to the essentials to afford oil or gas to heat their homes.

Brownouts were scheduled daily and blackouts became the norm; electricity was rationed like milk and butter.

Interestingly the entertainment industry continued to hang on as virtual reality became commonplace. Broadway theaters closed nearly all their doors immediately after the attack on New York.

White-collar workers, the hardest hit sector in the unemployment crisis were devastated by the attack. The effect on Wall Street was felt world round. Many a suit called it quits by one means or another; perhaps they finally learned that money could not buy everything, especially not security or protection from disaster. If they did not get it with the Enron scandal or the countless other white collar and corporate crimes then the terrorists taught them well and the hard way.

The numerous organized religions struggled, as much against the environmental changes as did the physical planet.

The American Catholic Church separated from Rome in late 2011. It was the Vatican's attempt to save the entire organization by means of amputation from what they considered an American problem, which became for them a gangrenous limb.

By 2009, 25 dioceses had filed for bankruptcy, resulting in countless churches being closed and boarded up. Between the years 1999-2009 millions of people left the church, feeling betrayed and angry over the abuse of children and the measures taken by the Council of Bishops to handle the matter in a more compassionate manner as well as the exclusion of the laity in the management of the affairs of the church.

Groups such as SNAP and Voice of the Faithful did what they could by forming factions with clergy members who were sympathetic and supportive of their cause, allowing the sacraments to go on. They celebrated mass in numerous places and one needed only to go the many boarded up churches to find a pamphlet tacked up on a nearby tree to find a location.

The Episcopal Church broke apart in the years 2004-2007. The inclusion of gays in their leadership was not tolerable and so they followed the early teachings of their faith, standing tall and confident of being right that it was what God had intended.

Many other religious organizations crumbled as well; the distant God created so long ago could not provide the needed comfort or remedy of the failures and suffering of humanity.

Now at the end of the year of 2012, the world was facing times like never before; most people didn't know what to do or what to think or say and only a few had planned for the times to come. The world that was meant to cradle humanity was changing rapidly and no one knew how to stop it; no one knew how to prepare for it. Duct tape and plastic would not shield them for what was coming.

On the 3rd of December of 2012 the family, now numbering in the hundreds, gathered in the meeting room waiting for Albert to speak. The children stood quietly behind Grace, knowing she too would speak to all present.

Albert began.

"As everyone knows, things are getting too difficult to manage. Food is getting harder to spread around, and we've can just double up and triple up in the rooms so much. We've outgrown our britches, as my ma would say. So, after much thought, discussion and investigating we have come to a decision that we want to present to you all tonight. Now, I know after hearing it, some of you will say no way, can't do it, and of course we understand, however, I want you know that you're all part of this and we invite you to go forward with us."

Ears perked up and eyes widened to pay full attention to the words to come. The room grew even more silent as all waited for Albert to continue.

"Two weeks ago, as you know Al Jr., Bob Whitely and young Grace went on a journey west. Who was leading, well that remains to be known, but what matters is the news that the three of them returned with, news I want to share with you now. They went west because that's where Grace was drawn; the child's spirit is strong and pure and seeks peace.

"They followed her lead and landed in a small town called Sweet Springs, Missouri, just about twelve hundred miles from here. They met up with two young men, brothers, when they stopped to eat at a diner in the center of town. From what I've been told, it was though they knew Grace was coming. They sat across from her in the booth and smiled head to toe, Al Jr. said, which leads me to believe they landed in the right spot.

"Anyway, after a lengthy conversation, the boys invited them back to their farm and well, this is the part that really kinda set the hairs standing straight up on my balding head. They showed the three what they had been working on for a year or two — several large housing structures, big enough to hold couple of hundred people easily. Nothing fancy, but comfy, practical, with showers, and cooking rooms, home like for sure. What amazed the two of them was that they weren't sure why they built the damn things, they just worked on 'em in between working the farm.

"So, where is all this leading? I can see some of you scratching your heads out there. Well, this is what I'm presenting to you tonight. We head out there, out to Sweet Springs. It will take a week or two to plan and get us all organized, but my heart tells me this is right, that this is our next step toward a place in our world that we want to live in and for those of us closer to the end than the beginning, a resting place.

"I know there must be lots of questions running threw your heads but I know Grace wants to say a few words, so I ask you to hold tight for a moment."

Grace walked up and stood in front of Albert. She raised her head, looked up at him as he took her hand and nodded for her to begin.

"When I sat across from Jodi and Jason I could feel that — just like all of you — they were part of this, of this moment in time. Jason looked at me, smiled, and didn't say a word but something inside let me know he knew I was coming, that we were coming and why.

"Too many things are happening here that tell me it's time to move on. I know that it will be scary and hard for some of you, but if you trust in what your heart tells you, you will be fine. You know already, what to do so trust that. Some might stay, and that is what is meant for them, for one reason or another, but I ask that whatever your choice let it be yours and allow everyone to make their own. This might mean children going and parents staying, but no matter what, I want you all to continue to hold fast to your *knowing* that the vision of a world of peace lies in their hearts. Hope in them, believe in them, and trust that what is the intention of the Creator for humanity lies in the heart of the children."

The crowd remained quiet and although questions were apparent on several faces, no hands went up at this moment.

Over the next several days, planning for the trip took place. This included securing the means of transportation, which ended up being numerous school buses that sat idle in a nearby lot as well as cars and vans owned by members of the family.

When it came time to create the list of all who were going to make the journey, Albert gathered them all together.

"Well, it's time — time to finalize whose coming and whose staying. Anyone who has thoughts, please feel free to speak up."

Helen Worthing, the eldest of the group step forward slightly from where she stood and spoke.

"Albert, we've talked this over, and we've made a the list of those going and those of us staying. Not because we don't want to go with you, but the reality of making a journey across country with so many is going to be a challenge to say the least. We all thought about it and came to know what to do. I'm old, Albert, I've got at least 20 years on you, and I know these old bones won't bounce kindly on the springs of a school-bus axle. And you'll note that some of the names are not of just us old folks. Some of us felt we could serve better if we remain to help out here. As soon as the rooms and beds empty out, they'll be filled with twice as many in need. You know this as well as I, so here you go, my dear friend, here's the list."

Helen walked forward and embraced Albert after handing him the list. Then she went on to Henna who took her in her arms to hold her tightly, knowing what a brave and selfless act so many were committing to. Helen whispered her words of love to Henna.

"Thank you, my dear, dear sister, thank you for giving me the chance to become part of the plan of God."

The next few days passed quickly as supplies were loaded and all vehicles were made ready. When the day of departure finally arrived, there were as many tears as there were smiles.

One young family stood apart the others.

"You listen to Henna and Albert, okay? And don't you worry about us, we're fine, we'll be just fine."

Rusty Appleton brushed the tears from young Sarah's face and held her tightly. His wife, Sharon, had her arms around them both.

"This is the best thing right now, honey. I'll stay with Daddy, so I can take care of him, and then when he's better we'll come out to be with you. So, don't think this is 'Goodbye' – it's just a 'So long, see ya later.' Okay? I love you Sarah, with all my heart. Make sure you stay close to Grace and Jeffrey and listen to what Henna tells you."

Sensing her presence needed, Henna went to them. She knelt down next to Sarah and lifted the faces of her weeping parents.

"You can trust that I will love and protect her as my own. No harm will come to your child, I swear to you both. And when you're stronger Rusty, you two will be able to see that for yourselves."

The buses and cars filled up with the anxious and somewhat heart aching travelers. It was the first day of 2013 and next part in the fulfillment of the plan of the Creator of All.

CIBOLA, NEW MEXICO

*G*yada sat in the belly of the cave looking upward into the beam of light that streamed from the heavens. Deep in trance, she chanted a mantra whose vibrations united with the light causing a shimmering display of splendor. A smile came upon her, and she nodded her head ever so slightly. Then she spoke to the heart of humanity, encouraging all to follow this child, her beloved Grace, who would lead them into an era of peace.

*M*any years ago, when I began my journey of learning my purpose, a wonderful therapist named Julie Bondi helped me to create a mantra that changed my inner thoughts of self-doubt and unworthiness. These words have evolved throughout the years until they formed as you read below and no doubt, they will evolve even more in the years to come. The journey to peace begins on a personal level perhaps now is your time to start.

I am one with the Creator; I am one with the Universe.
All the riches and the beauty of the Universe are here for me.
I release my past and look forward to glorious future.
I am harmony and balance, joy and prosperity, healing hands and words
I am Infinite Being, Infinite Wisdom and Infinite Love
I am one with the Creator; I am one with the Universe
I am peace.

Peace be with you,
Barbara Oleynick

Thank you to the entire staff of Phenix and Phenix and Synergy Books for assisting me in bringing this message to the world.